## "I WANT TO SPEND A LOT OF TIME WITH YOU," IAN SAID SOFTLY . . .

Kerry tried to ignore the warm, electric feeling that went through her as Ian's fingertips grazed her shoulder.

"Why don't you explore the city with me sometime, Kerry? You can even pick where we'll go."

Kerry sighed. "I told you I can't, Ian. I just don't have the time to go out."

"I know dancing is important to you, but I thought that I was, too."

"You are," she said. She was ridiculously close to tears. . . .

# *TURNING POINTS*

*A romance with two endings . . .
which one would you choose?*

(0451)

#1☐ **FRIENDS FOREVER by Lisa Norby.** ROMANCE OR
FRIENDSHIP? Laura liked Richie, the school's star quarter-
back, because he could always see the other person's side.
Lots of girls wanted to date him, and Laura didn't want to
lose him. But she didn't want to lose Katie, her best friend,
either. And even though Katie wasn't part of the football
crowd, didn't Laura owe her best friend some kind of loyalty
too? (129237—$1.25)*

#2☐ **KERRY'S DANCE by M.L. Kennedy.** THE BALLET OR
A BOYFRIEND? Kerry wanted to be a professional ballerina
more than anything in the world, until she met Ian. Then
she was running to classes, dancing until her muscles were
sore, and spending every spare minute with him. But the
pressure was too much, and Kerry knew something would
have to give. But would it be her first love, the ballet, or
her new love, Ian? (129245—$1.25)*

**Be sure not to miss the other *Turning Points* romances
in this exciting new Vista series.**

*Price is $2.50 in Canada

# Turning Points

## #2

# Kerry's Dance

by

## M.L. Kennedy

A SIGNET VISTA BOOK

**NEW AMERICAN LIBRARY**

PUBLISHED BY
THE NEW AMERICAN LIBRARY
OF CANADA LIMITED

## For Tara

PUBLISHER'S NOTE

This novel is a work of fiction. Names, characters, places, and incidents either are the product of the author's imagination or are used fictitiously, and any resemblance to actual persons, living or dead, events, or locales is entirely coincidental.

NAL BOOKS ARE AVAILABLE AT QUANTITY DISCOUNTS
WHEN USED TO PROMOTE PRODUCTS OR SERVICES.
FOR INFORMATION PLEASE WRITE TO PREMIUM MARKETING DIVISION,
NEW AMERICAN LIBRARY, 1633 BROADWAY,
NEW YORK, NEW YORK 10019.

RL5/IL5+

*Turning Points* is a trademark of New American Library.

First Printing, June, 1984

2  3  4  5  6  7  8  9

SIGNET VISTA TRADEMARK REG. U.S. PAT. OFF. AND FOREIGN
COUNTRIES REGISTERED TRADEMARK — MARCA REGISTRADA
HECHO EN WINNIPEG, CANADA

SIGNET, SIGNET CLASSIC, MENTOR, PLUME, MERIDIAN
and NAL BOOKS are published in Canada by The New American
Library of Canada, Limited, Scarborough, Ontario

PRINTED IN CANADA
COVER PRINTED IN U.S.A.

# Chapter 1

I'm fifteen years old, and like most people, I have my ups and downs. That's not a pun, incidentally, although my goal in life is to be a ballerina.

A lot of people have strange ideas about dancers. They expect us to be as powerful and sleek as racehorses, or as charming and fragile as china dolls. We're supposed to be beautiful and dazzling and defy the laws of gravity as we float across the stage in clouds of white tulle.

Sometimes we are.

On good days, when the adrenaline flows, I can glide and soar like a bird. On bad days, I think that if God had wanted us to stand with our toes pointing in opposite directions, he would have given us hinges and ball bearings instead of joints.

I guess I should begin at the beginning. My name is Kerry Graham, and ever since I was six years old, I have known exactly what I wanted to be. A classical dancer. I knew it, my parents knew it, and the word quickly spread among hordes of adoring relatives.

"Have you ever seen such talent?" my grandmother would ask anyone who would listen.

"Never! Not even on Rudolf Nureyev," was my grandfather's reply.

"And those pirouettes—she should be dancing on top of a music box," my Aunt Sylvie declared. This seemed like a totally impractical suggestion to me, but I took it as a compliment.

When I was six, my mother presented me with a bubble-gum pink leotard and a pair of stiff white ballet shoes.

When I was eight, my aunt bought me a scratchy, sequined tutu at Macy's, and I was on my way. Every Sunday afternoon, my mother would play "The Blue Danube" on the piano, while I galloped across the living room, pretending to be a world-famous ballerina. My relatives were enchanted. If they could have had their way, I would have immediately replaced the entire company of the New York City Ballet.

On my ninth birthday, I was a butterfly in Miss Talbot's spring recital, along with thirteen other little girls. My most vivid memory is of Miss Talbot standing in the wings, flapping her arms madly, urging all of us to "flutter."

When I was ten I staggered up *en pointe* and played a giant marshmallow in a children's theater production. My toes cracked and bled for sixth months straight, but I was making progress.

Thirteen was a bad year. I would have danced in *Sleeping Beauty* if it hadn't been for Shirley Markham. Shirley had the worst technique I've ever seen. Her *jetés* were terrible, but she had long blond hair and a smile that drove boys crazy. She grinned at the choreographer, and I knew that my fate was sealed.

For the past nine years, my life has revolved around classical ballet. Everything else—school, friends, eating, and sleeping—has been squeezed in between. At least I've always known exactly what to expect. Sometimes my life is so predictable, it reminds me of one of those giant pizza puzzles that come in tin cans. You can spread thousands of tiny pieces on the floor, but no matter how you rearrange the little chunks of mozzarella and tomato sauce, you always get the same thing: a giant pizza. No more, no less.

I always figured that was enough.

Until I met Ian MacDermott.

The 2:35 train screamed into the Bronxville station exactly ten minutes behind schedule. I groaned as I dashed across the platform with my duffle bag and books. I hoped the train would move out quickly. Whenever it was late, I was "tardy" for my ballet class in Manhattan, and Miss Beatrice gave me a look that would freeze my blood.

I threw myself into a window seat and took a deep breath. One thing at a time, I reminded myself. A half hour of concentrated study, and then it would be time for my three-hour dance class at the Academy.

I flipped open my Western Civilization book and got to work. Sometimes I was tempted to just close my eyes, lean back, and drift off to sleep like some of the other commuters, but I always had assignments to do. That day, for example, I had to study for a gigantic test over fifty pages of Western Civ.

7

That may not sound like much, but fifty pages in our textbook covered about three thousand years of history. In other words, everything from the invention of the wheel to the discovery of the Frisbee.

I was struggling with the dates of the Punic Wars when I heard a strange noise coming from the seat behind me. It reminded me of a large chipmunk. I tried to block it out of my thoughts and returned to my book.

Then there was a rattle of plastic, followed by a loud crunch. It sounded like . . . like . . . someone eating a Rubik's Cube.

Rattle. Crunch. Rattle. I held my breath. There was a long pause and then a violent crunch.

I whirled around furiously. "Can't you eat more quietly?" I hissed. Before the words were out of my mouth, I longed to take them back. Because I found myself staring into the most gorgeous gray eyes I had ever seen. Male eyes, fringed with incredibly black lashes. The eyes were part of a total package, of course—shiny blue-black hair, olive skin, and a set of dazzling white teeth.

"I'm trying to study," I said in a daze.

The boy looked at me with a grin. "Have a pistachio. Brain food, you know."

"No, thank you," I said. "I have to get back to work now." I turned away and buried my nose in my book, my cheeks flaming. No one should be that good-looking, I thought. It just isn't fair!

I felt a gentle tapping on the back of my seat. "I have Fritos, if you prefer," he said in a teasing voice.

"No thanks," I mumbled without turning around.

I heard a sigh from the seat behind me, but I ignored it. For a few minutes, there was dead silence, and I went back to trying to memorize all I could about the ancient Roman emperors. Miss Tyler had warned us that she might ask an essay question on them, so I read on about the system of aqueducts that the Romans built. It's amazing that they even had time to think about such things, since most of their time seemed to be spent boiling people in oil or eating seedless grapes.

"I even have gum," the voice said, and I nearly jumped. He had slid into the seat next to me. "Two kinds, raspberry and—"

"*Please* let me study," I begged him.

"Sugarless."

It was a standoff. He stared at me, and a slow smile started in his eyes and traveled to his mouth. I looked at him until I felt my face growing warm, then quickly looked down at my book.

Finally, he broke the silence. "My name's Ian MacDermott." He paused. "And now you're supposed to tell me your name," he said very seriously, as if he were talking to a five-year-old. When I didn't answer him, he said in a hurt voice, "Didn't your parents bring you up to be polite?"

"They certainly didn't bring me up to talk to strangers on the train."

"I'm not a stranger," he said with a grin. "I just introduced myself."

"All right," I said, giving in. "I'm Kerry Graham. And I'm sorry, but I'm very busy," I added, looking straight into those eyes.

"Hi, Kerry Graham-who-is-very-busy." He leaned over and read the title of my textbook. "Western Civ. How well I remember. I took that class last year. Need some help?"

"No."

"Let me give you a tip. They always ask the name of Caligula's horse."

"They do?" I was interested in spite of myself.

"Sure. And I bet you don't know it."

"Well—"

"He was a very important horse, you see. In fact, he was the first and only horse appointed to the Roman Senate. If you don't believe me, ask your teacher. I'm always interested in stuff like that," he said. "I'm kind of a trivia nut."

"I really do have to study," I said, but I wasn't sounding very convincing anymore.

He went right on talking. "I like Italian sports cars, pizzas with everything, and Billy Joel." He gave me another one of those heart-grabbing smiles. "Oh, and girls named Kerry." He paused for a moment and then nudged me. "Now it's your turn."

"Look, I really can't talk. I've got to study for a test tomorrow, and I only have"—I glanced at my watch—"thirteen minutes left to do it."

"Thirteen minutes! Do you do everything by the clock?"

"Well, I have to be organized," I said, feeling embarrassed. "Time is too precious to waste."

He frowned and pretended to be thinking. "Don't tell me. That's got to be either Ann Landers . . . or Alice Cooper."

"I don't know who said it," I snapped. "But it's

true. I have my day divided into one-hour segments, and I can account for every one of them."

"You can? I'm impressed."

"Yes, I can," I said, warming to the subject. "I'm in school for six hours a day, I dance for three hours, I spend an hour commuting . . ."

"What do you do for fun?"

I hesitated, and he looked at me in disbelief. "You must do *something* just for fun. Don't you ever go to movies, or the zoo, or wander around the city?" He stopped to cram another handful of pistachios in his mouth. For some reason, the noise didn't bother me anymore.

"I don't have much time," I said stiffly.

Ian rushed on as if I hadn't spoken. "Hey, do you take this train every day?"

I nodded. "I get on at Bronxville. I've got dance class in New York every afternoon from three-thirty to six-thirty."

"Fantastic. I get on at Tuckahoe, right before you. I'm a senior at Tuckahoe High and I finish work at six-thirty. I'm a page at a TV studio in New York. You know, a guide." His eyes looked excited. "I've got a great idea. Why don't you meet me after work tonight, and we'll grab a pizza?"

He grinned, and it was a smile that was guaranteed to melt stone. For a crazy moment, I was tempted. Then my sanity returned, and Miss Tyler's face floated in front of me as if someone had just rubbed a magic lamp.

"Sorry. I've got to study. And anyway, I always catch the train back to Bronxville right after class."

"I'll remember that." He smiled.

The train lurched to a stop, and I looked up, startled. Could the time have passed so quickly? I scrambled to my feet and collected my books.

Ian had thrown a sport coat over his pale blue shirt and was following me down the aisle. "Hey, don't I rate a good-bye?"

"It was nice to meet you," I said quickly. No matter how charming he was, I couldn't waste another minute—I was late as it was!

I dropped my duffel bag, and one of my leg-warmers tumbled out. Ian picked it up and looked it over. "What's this?" he asked.

"A leg-warmer." I quickly stuffed it back in the bag.

"A leg-warmer?" He hooted with laughter. "I thought it was a muffler for your pet giraffe."

"Very funny. And now, if you'll excuse me—" I tried unsuccessfully to push my way past a very fat lady in curlers blocking the aisle. I was about to change my strategy and go the other way when Ian suddenly bent his head down close to mine. We were standing just inches apart, and his breath was warm on my ear.

"Remember, " he whispered, "Caligula's horse." Then he winked and disappeared into the crowd.

Miss Beatrice, my ballet teacher, has the face of an angel and a voice that can cut glass. Someone once passed around a cartoon of glass shattering, with the caption: "Is it Beatrice, or is it Memorex?"

I was fifteen minutes late for class, and the rest of the girls were already at the barre doing *battements tendus.* I scurried to my place and hoped no one would notice me.

The studio was already stifling hot, even though

the skylight was open. Miss Beatrice was pounding a yardstick against the floor to keep time, and classical piano music tinkled somewhere in the background.

When she spotted me, she stopped counting and gave me a smile just like the one the Wicked Witch gave Dorothy. "So," she said nastily, "better late than never, Miss Graham." Originality was never one of her strong points.

"Sorry," I muttered. The other girls were swinging their legs in perfect time. A weaving line of waist-high kicks that were precise and controlled. I hadn't had time to warm up, and my muscles rebelled.

"I want to see a good turn-out," Miss Beatrice said, prodding my ankle with her yardstick. She moved on down the line, criticizing, encouraging, scolding, and never missing a beat of the music. "When I say I want your foot directly in front of your body, I mean directly in front of your body!" Her voice rose shrilly, and she kicked an offending foot into position. She had an amazing eye for design, and if someone was off by a millimeter, she knew it.

I glanced at Jill Abbott, and she winked at me. Physically, Jill and I are opposites—she has long blond hair, like a princess, and my hair is dark and curly. But we had one important thing in common—ballet was our whole life. Neither one of us was overly fond of Miss Beatrice, but we both admired her as a dancer.

My concentration was off, and I wondered why. Usually I get so wrapped up in dancing that I block everything else out of my mind. Dancing is impossibly hard work and takes undivided attention. If you watch a group of dancers practicing, you'll see that their faces look tense, and their neck muscles stand out in tight ridges. We save our smiles for the audience.

After an hour of barre work, we moved to the center of the floor to practice steps and combinations. We were working on *jetés* today—those fantastic leaps that look like scissor kicks suspended in midair—but nothing was going right. The idea in a *jeté* is to leap effortlessly and land lightly on the balls of the feet, ready to spring again. I was lumbering through my third try at being light and graceful when the yardstick cracked warningly on the floor.

"Lightly! Lightly! Think of a feather, Kerry. You're landing like a sack of potatoes," Miss Beatrice yelled.

I bungled my way through another hour of practice, and then it was finally time for a break. I was waiting to buy a diet drink, when Jill walked over to me.

"Having an off day?" she asked sympathetically. She was wearing a bright red leotard, navy blue sweat shorts, and a wide yellow belt that made her look like Wonder Woman.

"I guess so," I admitted.

"Not having trouble with bunions again, are you?"

I shook my head. Dancers are cursed with every kind of foot problem known to human beings— bunions, corns, and calluses are just a few—and sometimes I feel like a walking ad for Dr. Scholl's.

Jill started to ask what was wrong when Miss Beatrice crept up behind us like a cat.

"Dancers dance with their heads, not their feet," she announced. This was one of her favorite sayings, and she never missed a chance to repeat it. "The brain tells the feet what to do," she said flatly. "Remember that, Graham."

"I will," I promised, and Jill grinned and rolled her eyes at me.

A few minutes later, the bell sounded, and we were back in the studio. I thought over what Miss Beatrice had said. I hated to admit it, but she was absolutely right. The problem wasn't my feet; it was my head.

For the first time in my life, I had let myself be distracted by . . . trivia. But such good-looking trivia! I thought of Caligula and his horse and smiled.

# Chapter 2

I had a feeling I would see Ian on the train that night. My hands were clammy from excitement as I dashed through Grand Central Station just in time to catch the 6:50. I threw myself into a window seat—to make it easier for him to spot me—and tried to calm the quivery feeling in my stomach.

Where could he be? I scanned the crowd on the platform and forced myself to take a few deep breaths. My heart was beating out a crazy disco rhythm in my chest, and I could feel a goofy grin spreading over my face. Call it what you want—feminine intuition or ESP—I just knew he would be there!

It's a good thing I don't have to make my living as a psychic because my instincts were totally wrong. Ian never showed up.

When the train finally gave a warning belch and pulled out of the station, I heard a rustling noise in the seat behind me. I whirled around happily. "So there you are!"

I was startled to see four hostile eyes glaring at me. "Oops, sorry," I muttered, as the sailor and his girl friend went back to their clinch. For the next few minutes, their soft laughter was more irritating than Ian and his pistachios had been.

I sighed and began to explore the mysteries of American Civics when a tiny blue-haired lady dropped into the seat next to me. A tiny, *talkative* blue-haired lady.

"Have you given much thought to the end of the world, my dear?" she began, smiling at me in a friendly way.

"Not lately," I said. I tried to slide down in my seat like a hermit crab retreating into its shell. "I've been kind of busy." As if to prove it, I flipped open my textbook and pretended to be fascinated by the chapter on the Johnson presidency. Unfortunately, the only interesting thing in the whole section was a footnote testifying that LBJ ate more pork barbecue than any president in recent memory. That was exactly the type of question Miss Gibbons would ask in a multiple-choice test, and I decided to underline it.

"We're all busy," the lady continued. "But we can't be too busy to ignore something as monumental as the destruction of the universe." She settled an enormous shopping bag on the seat between us and smiled.

"I suppose not," I said doubtfully, still wishing Ian would magically appear.

"There isn't much time left, you know." That got my attention, and I stared hard at her. "The end is almost here," she added ominously. She leaned forward and snatched my hand with a surprisingly strong grip. "You had better be prepared," she hissed, and I noticed that her eyes were unnaturally bright. She continued to hold my hand in her viselike clutch as she reached into the shopping bag.

What if she has a gun! I thought. She could hijack the whole train to . . . where was the end of the line? If I missed ballet class for even one day, Miss Beatrice would never forgive me. She always claimed that the only valid excuse for missing class was a death in the family—preferably one's own.

"I'm sorry, but I have to go now," I said, jumping to my feet.

"But time is running out," she pleaded. She dug her fingers painfully into my wrist and tried to force a pamphlet into my hand.

I managed to pry off her fingers one by one and darted into the aisle. She immediately turned to the seat behind her. "Excuse me," I heard her say to the sailor. "Have you given much thought to where you'll spend eternity?"

I never heard his answer because I began a lurching journey through all fourteen cars of the train, looking for Ian. In the sixth car, I thought I spied his shiny dark hair. When I bent down, a middle-aged man in the aisle seat scowled at me, and his companion gave a rude laugh.

It was hopeless. Maybe Ian MacDermott didn't exist at all. Maybe I had made him up in my dreams.

I was starving hungry when I got home. The Wizard was parked in front of the television devouring his favorite snack—a marshmallow-chocolate-chip-graham cracker sandwich. The rest of the family is into nutrition, but the Wizard is a

Twinkie fan. He swears that if Mom donated one of her eggplant casseroles to CARE, the starving natives would send it right back.

The Wizard isn't too bad a kid, if you're into twelve-year-old brothers. As far as I'm concerned, they're strictly an acquired taste—like olives or pickled onions.

His real name is Daniel, but we call him the Wizard because he's really smart. He'll never have to study as hard as I do. His teachers have given him dozens of intelligence and personality tests over the years, and he manages to outwit them every time.

"Some guy called you," he mumbled, as I stepped over him. His eyes never left the set. He was watching *I Love Lucy* reruns, which doesn't indicate great genius to me, but then, I'm not a psychologist. The Wizard is a television junkie, and he laughed hysterically as Lucy danced inside a vat of grapes.

"Who was it?"

"Huh?" said the genius.

"Who called?" I turned down the volume on the set. The Wizard continued to stare at the screen, unfazed.

"Who called?" I repeated impatiently. I stepped in front of the set, a human barrier, and was happy to see that he blinked and frowned. Even geniuses don't have X-ray vision, and *I Love Lucy* was his favorite show.

"I told you, some guy," he answered between bites.

"Well, didn't he leave a name?"

"Oh, yeah. Ian Fleming or something like that."

19

Ian! He'd called! He was real after all. Maybe he'd taken an earlier train.

I floated into the kitchen and nearly fainted from the delicious smell of roast beef and baked potatoes. "Mom," I protested, "don't do this to me. You know I've got to keep my weight down for dancing."

"A few potatoes never hurt anyone." She smiled.

"That's what Gina's mother told her," I complained. Gina's mother's cooking was almost her downfall. She put on so much weight that she went up to a hundred and thirty pounds, and Miss Beatrice suspended her from the company for months. The male dancers complained that when they lifted her into the air, it was like hoisting a sack of wet cement.

"And Miss Beatrice—"

"Miss Beatrice can't see every bite you eat," Mom said, as she put the tempting dinner in front of me.

"She'd like to," I muttered, as I sat down.

"You look tired," she said, brushing my hair out of my eyes.

"A little," I told her. "I've got a Western Civ. test coming up, and there's a term paper due that I haven't even started."

She poured herself a cup of coffee and sat next to me. "Well, don't overdo it, honey. I know how hard it is for you to keep up with your schoolwork, with your schedule." Then, luckily, she changed the subject.

"Anything special happen today?" She picked up a fork and began idly tracing a design on the tablecloth.

"I finally got that *arabesque* down pat. Remember how my leg used to tremble? It's steady now, and straight as a board."

"That's great! I know you worked hard on it."

I put some extra sour cream on my potato, deciding to go for broke. I'd do an extra half hour at the barre, hoping Miss Beatrice wouldn't notice.

"I met someone on the train today," I began slowly.

She looked at me curiously. "From the look on your face, he was pretty interesting." My mother never missed anything.

"He was," I said, grinning. "I just thought I'd mention it in case he calls. In fact, I think he already has, and the Wizard took the message. His name is Ian MacDermott."

"Ian MacDermott . . . what a marvelous name," she said dreamily. "He sounds like he should be the hero in a Gothic novel. I can just picture a tall, dark, mysterious stranger . . . someone terribly moody who spends hours brooding on a Scottish heath. Does he live in Bronxville?"

"No, he's a senior from Tuckahoe, and he works at a TV studio in New York every day after school."

"There has to be more," she teased.

"There is!" I laughed. "You were partly right. He's tall and handsome, but he's not moody—he's got a terrific personality, and he's probably the most interesting boy I've ever met." And I'll probably never get a chance to see him again, with my crazy schedule, I added to myself.

We gabbed for a few more minutes, and then it was time for me to dash upstairs and finish some assignments. It seems that no matter how organized I am, or how hard I try, I'm always falling behind in something.

I did ten minutes of *pliés* to ward off a charley horse I had felt coming on in dance class, and then fell into an exhausted sleep.

Ian's face drifted in and out of my thoughts all the next day. There was no use kidding myself. I could hardly wait to see him again!

I was busily writing his name over and over in different kinds of letters when Mr. Tilson called on me.

"Who would like to identify an atom that carries a positive or negative charge as a result of losing or gaining an electron? How about you, Miss Graham?"

"Ian," I said by mistake. "I mean, *ion*," I hastily corrected myself. Luckily, Mr. Tilson didn't notice anything strange, and he went back to discussing the mysteries of atomic orbits and molecular bonding.

As a special treat, he dragged out one of his famous audiovisual aids. It was a black-and-white film from the 1950s, and we groaned at the corny title: *I Am a Chemical*. The sound track had a high-pitched whine like a vacuum cleaner, and a man in a crewcut told us in a very serious voice that the human body consists of ninety-eight cents worth of chemicals. Everyone nearly fainted from boredom, but you could tell Mr. Tilson was really excited over this movie. "Imagine!" he said in an amazed voice. "The human body is worth only ninety-eight cents! It boggles the mind!" Luckily the bell rang just then, and we could escape to lunch.

"What did you think of Tilson today?" Shauna asked, as we stood in the cafeteria line. Shauna Monroe is my closest friend in high school, even though we don't have many classes together.

Marla Peters answered her question. "That man gets more boring every day. And that movie—a total gross-out." Marla had had it in for Mr. Tilson ever since the day he caught her writing letters in class.

I hesitated over the steaming counter, watching enviously as Shauna ordered the lasagne special. She ate like a truck driver and never gained an ounce.

I wandered over to the salad bar and looked over the limp lettuce and wilted vegetables. "Maybe I'll just have some cottage cheese and a pear," I said to the woman working there.

"Are you still on a diet, Kerry?" Marla asked. "You're going to waste away."

"She's supposed to be thin," Shauna said defensively. "She has to be thin for her career."

"Oh, her career," Marla said, drawing the word out to five syllables and giggling. Marla was not the most serious person in our school. She spent a lot of time giggling. I just ignored her. It wasn't worth explaining how important my dancing was. She would never understand.

Shauna and I sat at the far corner of the table. "Notice anything different about me?" she asked.

I stared at her, looking for something new. Same long auburn hair and green eyes, same sprinkling of freckles that even nightly treatments with lemon juice couldn't erase.

"Look!" she said impatiently. She pushed back her thick hair, and I saw that she was wearing white and gray feathers on each ear. "Feather earrings," she said proudly. "Aren't they darling? Tell me the truth, Kerry," she said, tucking her hair behind her ears so I could get the full effect, "are they 'me,' or not?"

"Nice," I said, trying to smile. I would never have chosen earrings like that for myself, but I had to admit they looked pretty dramatic on Shauna.

"I love feather earrings," Bunny Adams said, plunking her tray down next to ours.

As she and Shauna began comparing their earring collections, I opened my English book, and let the conversation wash over me. During my freshman year, I used to get teased about studying at lunchtime, but by now everyone was used to it. I missed out on a lot of fun sometimes, but it was the only way I could get by in school and keep up with my dance schedule.

"So what are you wearing to the dance on Friday?" Marla asked Bunny.

"Oh, wait till you see. Bud is going to love how I look in my new outfit."

Bunny liked clothes that were tight, black, and sequined. Preferably all three. That day she was wearing her favorite school outfit: a halter knit top, tight jeans, and lots of gold jewelry.

As she described her new outfit in detail, I turned my attention back to English. Now I had to study harder than ever at lunch because I wanted to make sure that my time on the train would be free for Ian. For a full minute, though, I let my mind wander, and it invented a delicious fantasy: I would invite Ian to the dance on Friday, I would wear something gorgeous and spend the evening in his arms . . .

I was jolted back to the present when I realized that I had to read sixty pages before the test. So much for romance! I sighed and went back to work.

With any luck, I'd see Ian the next day.

# Chapter 3

"I've been thinking about you and Uncle Herman," Ian said suddenly. We were barreling through the upper Bronx on the trusty local, and the afternoon sun was doing a shadow dance over his movie-star features.

"Me and Uncle Herman?" I hadn't a clue what he was talking about.

"Herman Melville," he said, tapping my copy of *Moby Dick*. "I know you've been worried about your term paper, but thanks to me, your problems are over."

"They are? I'm happy to hear it," I said. I had been struggling with my research for three weeks solid, and I was beginning to see why Melville said it was tough to get poetry out of blubber. "And what, may I ask, is your brilliant idea?"

"Listen to the title I've got for you: 'From Moby Dick to Orca—the Revenge of the Mammals.' "

"Who in the world is Orca?"

"You've never heard of Orca?" He slapped his

forehead in mock amazement. "How can you stand living such a sheltered life? Don't you ever go to the movies?"

"I told you, I never have the time," I said in a small voice.

"*Orca* is one of the film classics of all time. It's got everything—love, hate, jealousy . . . terror." He gestured wildly and almost knocked off his sunglasses. "It's about this fantastic killer whale who goes on a rampage and terrorizes a small New England village."

"It sounds absolutely fascinating," I said sarcastically.

"It is," he said. "It's like Moby Dick in reverse. You see, Orca is out for revenge because Richard Harris killed his wife."

"Richard Harris killed his wife?"

"Killed Orca's wife. Mrs. Orca."

"Oh, I see." I didn't, but it was easier to pretend that I did.

"Well, it was really an accident. Richard Harris plays a sea captain who's hired to capture specimens of marine biology. His first mate harpoons Orca's pregnant wife by mistake, and that's where the feud begins. I'm really surprised you've never heard of it. It won the Worst Mammal Movie Ever Made award."

"Ian, you're hopeless." I smiled at him.

"Hopeless! Some gratitude," he said, pretending to be annoyed. "I've got it all planned. We can go see it tomorrow night. It's playing at a little theater on Seventy-sixth Street, and there's a great restaurant right next door." He looked so happy—and so pleased with himself for having planned the perfect date. "I'll pick you up at six."

"Ian, I can't go. I've got dance class."

"All right, then we'll go to the eight o'clock show. There's a double feature, so we can see *Return of the Gut-Slitters* instead. I hate to miss *Orca*, though," he said wistfully.

"Ian, I'd better not. I've got to get home and work on my term paper. Honestly. I'm so far behind as it is."

"But tomorrow's Friday night! And, besides, this will be educational, I swear!" He held up his hand like a boy scout taking the pledge. "It's a nature film, and it's even recommended by the National Geographic Society."

"Ian—"

"Okay, so maybe I exaggerate a little. Anyway, I'll make a movie buff out of you yet," he promised, "but I can see that it's going to be uphill work."

We talked nonstop for the rest of the ride, and I realized that Ian was interested in a lot of things. Besides being a horror-movie fan—he had seen thirty-six of the "Fifty Worst Movies Ever Made"—he knew a lot about pop art and rock music. He was athletic, too, and had won a medal in track at his high school. After talking to Ian, I felt like I had spent the last fifteen years living in a shell.

"What do you do on Sundays?" he said abruptly.

"The usual. I do an hour of barre work before breakfast, spend the morning working on dance routines, and study in the afternoon."

"That's really the way you spend your day? Don't you do anything for fun? It sounds awful," he said, making a face. "Like you're programmed. You always know what's coming next."

"I don't mind it," I said. "I can accomplish more that way."

"Maybe." He looked doubtful. "I guess we're opposites, Kerry. I like to stay loose. In fact, I'm probably the most unstructured person I know. Sometimes when I'm faced with two choices, and they both look good, I just flip a coin. I learned that trick from my mother."

It sounded like a pretty bizarre idea to me, but I didn't want to insult him and say so.

"Your mother really told you to flip a coin when you're faced with a decision?"

"Yeah, she's an artist, and she's also the most laid-back mother in the world. You see, the whole idea in flipping the coin is that you don't have to accept the answer." I must have looked puzzled, because he said quickly, "Suppose you have two choices, A and B, and you don't know which you really want to do. You flip a coin, and you tell yourself that if it comes up heads, you'll choose A, and tails, you'll choose B. Okay. You flip the coin, and it comes up A. Now all you have to do is ask yourself how you feel. If you're happy, then you really wanted it to be A all the time. But if you're disappointed, then you really wanted it to be B. It's a snap, because it forces you to confront your choices." He moved in a little closer to me and flashed a big smile. "You should try it sometime."

"I . . . I'll think about it," I stammered. I was starting to feel a little uncomfortable because Ian had put his arm on the top of my seat, and it was moving down toward my shoulders. "You asked me about Sundays," I said quickly, changing the subject. "What do you do on Sundays?"

"I just close my eyes and pick something exciting to do," he said with a laugh.

"You mean you imagine something?"

"No. I literally close my eyes and let my finger run down the entertainment listings in the paper. Just like a roulette wheel—where it stops nobody knows!"

"Then what?"

"Then I take off. You wouldn't believe some of the things I've gone to." He grinned. "I've ended up at an art auction at Parke Bernet, a chamber music concert at the Cloisters . . . let's see, I went to a street festival in Chinatown, and once I almost got arrested at a protest march in Washington Square."

"That was listed as entertainment?"

"No, I was looking for a poetry reading at a coffee house on MacDougal Street, and I got side-tracked."

He let his fingertips graze my shoulder, and I tried to ignore the warm, electric feeling that went through me. "Why don't you come on one of my expeditions with me, Kerry? I'll even let you pick the place," he said.

"I told you I can't, Ian. I just don't have the time." Miss Beatrice always says that dancing involves sacrifice, and this must be one of them, I thought unhappily. I felt close to tears. "Will I see you on the way home tonight?"

"Afraid not. We're having a birthday party at Mama Leone's for one of the pages. Want to come?"

"I'd like to, but—"

"But duty calls. I know," he said, cutting me off. We pulled into Grand Central Station, and Ian stood up and gave a little shrug. "Well, if they ever let you out on bail, you know where to find me."

"Bail! You make me sound like a prisoner." I tried for a light touch, but it didn't quite come off.

"You are, Kerry. And you don't even know it," he said softly. He stared at me for a long moment, and then turned and melted into the crowd.

I stood rooted to the spot, too shaken to follow him.


It was audition night for *Swan Lake*, and the reception room overflowed with dancers in colorful tights. They sprawled gracefully on the battered sofas and chairs, and draped their long legs over Formica coffee tables. A few sat in impossible positions on the floor.

"Nothing to worry about. It's the same old faces again," Inga Swenson concluded. All of Miss Beatrice's regular students were jealous of the "outsiders" who came to auditions. A ballet company is a closed society and dancers aren't known for their tolerance of newcomers—especially when there aren't enough parts to go around for everyone.

"Alison Chambers is here," I said. "I heard she did some Off-Broadway work last month."

Inga followed my gaze and eyed her suspiciously. Alison Chambers was a sexy brunette in a shocking-pink body suit. She stood in the center of the room, poised on one foot like a glamorous flamingo.

Inga sighed and tossed her long blond ponytail

over her shoulder. At five-foot ten, she was easily the tallest member of the group and one of the most beautiful.

I was going to question her further when Miss Beatrice appeared next to us.

"Hurry, girls, we need to start class!" She bustled around the room and shepherded us into the studio as if we were a flock of geese.

As soon as my shoes hit the polished wooden floor, I felt a familiar rush of happiness and excitement. This is exactly where I belong, I thought gratefully.

I loved almost everything about dancing. I loved the way the music pounded through the floor and made my toes tingle, the impossible leaps and turns that left me suspended in midair like a bird—even the endless repetitions at the barre that made my muscles quiver.

Miss Beatrice said that it took more than talent to be a classical dancer; it took guts, hard work, and sacrifice. I thought briefly of Ian and then forced him out of my mind.

"Wow, I missed the bus," Jill panted, as she dropped to the floor beside me. She reached into her tote bag and fumbled for her satin toe shoes.

"Toe shoes?" We never wore toe shoes for class.

"I'm auditioning for *Swan Lake*," she explained. "But the minute the audition is over, I'll come back to class. It's okay, Miss Beatrice knows about it." She began stuffing little chunks of lamb's wool between her toes, and I noticed that her feet were a chiropodist's dream—a mass of bunions and ugly swellings. She stared at me.

"Aren't you going to try out?"

I hesitated. I already had more than I could handle. "When are rehearsals?"

"Right after class, so there's no problem. And it's only a few nights a week, from six-thirty to eight-thirty. Are you sure you don't want to come? There are only a few more nights of auditions."

"I'll think about it," I promised. If I worked on *Swan Lake*, I'd miss the early train to Bronxville and would never get to see Ian. I wouldn't get to see his gorgeous eyes or hear his fabulous laugh all the way home . . .

Miss Beatrice's voice jolted me back to the present. "You all know where to start," she snapped. "*Battements tendus.*"

Within a few minutes, I was caught up in the rhythm of the warm-ups. Miss Beatrice always gave us exactly the same routine, and I could almost put my mind on automatic pilot and do it.

Slide the toe forward on the floor, directly to the front. Slide it back, and go to the side. Slide it back and go behind. Repeat. Repeat. Change sides . . .

Miss Lili, Miss Beatrice's assistant, shouted commands like a drill sergeant. "One, two, three, and four. Stay . . . and stay . . . and stay," she pleaded, as legs trembled in midair and neck muscles stood out like stalks of celery.

We had just moved to the center of the floor to work on combinations when Jill darted into place next to me. She looked pale but triumphant, and I knew that she had done well. She flashed an "OK" sign, and I grinned back at her.

Jill was born to dance; there was no question about it. Thin and intense, she put in longer hours than anyone else in the company and never complained. She was even applying for a scholarship to study ballet in Paris. She told me once that she was "centered," which means that she had freed her mind from distractions and could concentrate totally on dancing.

I watched her as she moved effortlessly across the floor, and felt a twinge of envy. Her future was secure; she was safe and sure of herself in the world of dance. She had a clear path, with no compromises or regrets. What a wonderful position she was in . . .

I used to be just like her, I told myself. Until I met Ian.

# Chapter 4

"I'm in *Swan Lake!*" Jill screamed when class was over. She gave me a hug and did a little dance around the dressing room. "I can't believe it. I'm playing a peasant girl, and I'm also an understudy for one of the cygnets!"

"The cygnets?"

"The four cygnets, remember? They do the precision number that always brings down the house."

I remembered. The cygnets were the equivalent of teen-age swans, who linked arms and did a Rockette-style dance in Act Two. It always reminded me of matinee time at Radio City Music Hall, but the audiences loved it.

"They may get John Martin for the Prince. Oh, Kerry, he's fabulous. He started doing his *grands jetés* in the wings, and by the time he hit center stage, he was practically airborne. Even the audition audience clapped, and you know how unusual that is. He was electrifying!" She stared dreamily at herself in the wall mirror, lost in a star-struck reverie over John and his *jetés*.

I was about to ask her about the rehearsal schedule when she snapped back to life. "And Odile! You're not going to believe who they've cast for the part. They're doing double casting, of course, and the same dancer plays Odette. Tell me, if you could choose anyone in New York to handle a double role like that, who would you choose?"

"Natalie Petrov, but she's in Europe . . ."

"No, she's back, and Mr. Rudikoff has signed her. Sometime during rehearsal, I'm going to ask her to show me how she does those *fouettés*. I'll beg, if I have to."

"I don't think you'll have to resort to that." I laughed. "I met Natalie once here at the studio, and she was really nice. She didn't come on like a prima ballerina at all. And if you find out the secret of those *fouettés*, be sure to clue me in, okay?" A *fouetté* is a sort of whipping turn on one leg, and if it's done right, it can be a real applause-getter. In *Swan Lake*, Odile, the Black Swan, does thirty-two *fouettés* in a row, because she's so thrilled at having outwitted the Prince. The dancer who plays the role practically has to be a human top.

The Prince, not to be outdone, does a wild series of *jetés* to show his uncontrollable excitement at finding his lady love. Classical dancers tend to express great passions by leaping in the air, which would be considered strange in real life, but is normal in ballet.

"Anyway, Kerry, you've just got to try out. It's the chance of a lifetime." She looked at me, flushed and happy, and I had to admit that I was getting excited over the idea.

"There are some swan parts left," she said, as if I

needed some extra persuasion. "Or you could be one of the six girls who dance with the Prince, or there's a part left in the Polish mazurka . . ."

"Okay, okay," I said, laughing a little. "You win, Jill. I'll audition, but how I'll fit in the rehearsals, I don't know."

"It's no problem," she said breezily. "You'll be here at the studio every day for class, anyway, so just plan on staying a couple of extra hours." She gave a little jump to get into her skin-tight designer jeans, and ran a brush through her gorgeous hair. "Now, let's get a bite to eat to celebrate. I'm starving!"

I sighed. Jill's snacks usually involved between three- and four-thousand calories. Like Shauna, she never gained an ounce, and relied on sheer nervous energy to keep slim.

We made a quick trip to a nearby ice cream place for a chocolate shake, and I explained to Jill that I had to be home early to hit the books.

"I don't know how you do it, Kerry," she said as she scooped up a dollop of whipped cream. "When I get home, all I want to do is fall into bed. Well, here's to both of us," she said, "and to a wildly successful performance."

"Cheers." We clinked glasses and giggled. "Of course, you realize that I may not even get a part," I reminded her.

"Oh, you will. I just know it." She gave a little silvery laugh that sounded like temple bells. "Mr. Rudikoff is going to be terrific to work with," she said happily. "He was absolutely brilliant at the audition. He said that *Swan Lake* is the most beautiful, lyrical ballet ever written. Oh, you'll just love him, Kerry. He said to think of our arms as violins. Can you imagine?"

I couldn't, but I tried to look impressed. I had met Mr. Rudikoff only once, and he reminded me of a pint-sized Kris Kringle.

"How did most of the dancers look?"

"Alison was terrible," Jill said with obvious pleasure. "She was enough of an egomaniac to audition for the lead, and she bombed. I wish you could have seen her darting all over the stage flapping her arms. She looked like a pigeon hunting for bread crumbs, instead of a dying swan. Mr. Rudikoff watched her for about thirty seconds and then yelled, 'Next!' I think she was crushed. She's going to realize that she needs more than a pink bodysuit to land a part," she said with grim satisfaction. Then she went on to tell me all about a ballet she had seen that weekend with her parents.

I nodded politely, only half-listening, because my mind was really with Ian. He's at Mama Leone's this very minute, I told myself, and I could just picture him laughing and talking with his friends. Probably a girl friend. He'd be sitting close to her and flashing one of those heart-grabbing smiles over the pasta. It's tough to look soulful and romantic eating spaghetti, but if anyone could manage it, Ian could. I let my mind wander, catching only snatches of Jill's conversation.

"Her *arabesques* were fantastic . . . but her *développés* needed some work . . . if you like speed instead of precision, I guess she was okay . . ."

I made a loud slurping noise when I hit the bottom of my shake, and it jolted me back to reality.

Jill was staring at me, and a frown was creasing her lovely features.

"Are you all right, Kerry?" She looked worried and a little annoyed. I could hardly blame her. I had been tuned out for quite a while.

"Sure I am. Why do you ask?" I blustered. I wondered exactly how long I had been daydreaming.

"Well, you've been acting kind of funny lately. I don't want to sound like a teacher, but your timing was way off in class again tonight. You'll never make it in a *pas de deux* if you get sloppy with your timing and technique."

"You're right. I stepped on Lisa's foot during that *pas de bourrée* sequence," I muttered. Although to be perfectly frank about it, I thought that Lisa had overreacted by giving a very unprofessional yelp.

Jill's face softened, and she said gently, "Hey, I'm only telling you this because I'm your friend. You'd rather hear it from me than Miss Beatrice, wouldn't you?"

"Definitely." I managed a weak laugh. "I'll just have to buckle down. Maybe more practice at the barre will do the trick." Or more concentration, I added silently.

"What do you think the problem is? We've always been neck and neck in ballet up till now."

She was right. Jill had started ballet at the same time that I had, and our friendly competition had spurred each of us to do our best. Our legs had quivered through *développés* together and trembled through *grands battements*. We had even bought our first pair of pink satin toe shoes together. I remembered how we had raced back to my room to try them out, only to discover that humans weren't meant to stand on their toes after all. Trying to balance the human body on a tiny square of wood hidden in a toe shoe is like trying to get an elephant to dance on a wastebasket. We managed to stand on our tiptoes for just a few seconds before tumbling into an ungraceful heap on the floor.

"Please, Kerry, put everything you can into this audition. I really want you to be in *Swan Lake* with me."

"I really want to be in it, too," I told her as we got up to pay the bill. But how in the world will I ever manage it? I wondered.

My mother wondered exactly the same thing.

I was slaving over my Melville term paper later that night, when she tapped on the door. "Break time," she said softly, handing me a cup of lemon-spiced tea. "Maybe this will get you going," she added, putting a plate of chocolate-chip cookies on my desk. She knew I could never resist homemade cookies, even though they are a forbidden treat. Miss Beatrice likes her dancers thin—so thin you can almost see their bones jutting through the flimsy leotards.

"You're tempting me." I smiled at her.

"Well, you'll need some fuel if you're going to work this hard. But you really should think about calling it a day pretty soon, Kerry. It's almost ten." She stared at the mountain of books and papers. "How come you're so swamped? Usually you stay on top of everything."

She was right. Shauna says that I am the most

disgustingly organized person she has ever met. I have an appointment book, an assignment pad, and a giant wall calendar that lets me see what's going on for the next twelve months. Shauna swears it's the most depressing thing she has ever seen, but I love it. You can write on it with a Magic Marker, but it's erasable, so it will last forever.

"But what happened?" my mother wanted to know.

"I don't know," I hedged. "I planned on spending three days on a rough draft for this term paper, and it's stretching into a week . . . I'm behind in my reading for two other classes, and I've got a test on quadratic equations tomorrow."

I glanced at my assignment pad. There was no way I could get to bed before midnight, and that would make the third time this week.

"Are you sure you're not being a perfectionist, Kerry? You know, trying too hard?"

"Mom, I'm not doing any extra, believe me. It's just getting harder for me to keep up with everything. In fact, at the rate I'm going, I'm sure some of my grades are going to fall this semester."

"Perish the thought!" My father was standing in the doorway holding his overcoat. He kissed my mother and then gave me a quick hug.

"I'd almost given up on you, Dan," she said. "What's left of your dinner is cremating in the broiler-oven."

"Now, Cynthia, you know I can't keep regular hours." He gave her a winning smile, and I could see her weakening. "What's this nonsense your grades slipping?" he said, pretending to be stern.

"Math may do me in," I told him.

"Math wasn't my best subject either," he admitted. "That's why I had to go into criminal law instead of taxation." He sat on the edge of my bed. "I haven't seen you since . . . when? Tuesday?"

"At least." My father is a workaholic, but I'm crazy about him anyway. He goes into his office before I'm even out of bed and hardly ever joins us for dinner. In fact, I rarely ever see him at night, unless I make an effort to wait up for him.

"Everything okay, honey?"

"It's fine, Dad." I smiled to reassure him, and he stood up wearily. "Well, I'll just check in on the Wizard before I get a bite to eat, ladies."

"I'll be right down, Dan," Mom said. After he left, she stared hard at me. "Kerry Graham, you look terrible. Really washed-out."

"Maybe it's the lights," I said.

She shook her head. "It's more than that. Are you sure you're not taking on too much? It wouldn't be the end of the world if you eased up on the studying a little, you know."

"Mom! You're not supposed to say things like that."

"Well, I did," she said firmly.

"Maybe you better get Dad's dinner," I said, trying to change the subject. Parents can go on forever once they get started on a subject, and I had tons of homework left to do.

"That's all right. A few minutes more won't make any difference." She pulled up a chair, and I could see that there was a major discussion coming on.

"I think you're pushing too hard, Kerry," she said softly.

"I'm not—"

"You are," she cut in quietly. "If you spend all your time worrying about achievements, you're going to end up like a robot. After all, you've got to leave some time for fun. These are supposed to be the best years of your life."

"I'll remember that," I kidded her. The best years of my life! My eyes felt like someone had rubbed sand into them, and every aching muscle was sending out an SOS.

"What ever happened to your friend on the train? I thought you might like to invite him over sometime."

"I never have the time, Mom. In fact, he asked me out tonight to celebrate a friend's birthday, but there was just no way I could go."

"It's too bad he didn't ask you out on a weekend. He sounds like a very special young man, and I'd like to meet him."

"He did," I said sadly. "And I had to turn him down again."

"Isn't that playing a little too hard to get? Kerry, you really should have some more friends—some life beyond the dance studio."

"Well, I'll be really busy for the next few weeks, anyway. I didn't have a chance to tell you, but I'll be auditioning for *Swan Lake* tomorrow night."

"*Swan Lake*! How will you fit it in your schedule?"

I didn't dare tell her I had wondered the same thing. "They're only doing one act, not three," I said to pacify her. "And it won't be so bad," I added, parroting Jill. "After all, rehearsals are right after class, so it will just mean I'll be getting home around nine o'clock, instead of seven."

I managed to sound a lot more casual than I really felt. I had to admit that I was always exhausted lately, dragging myself from school to the studio to the library to home. Still, I reminded myself, how many kids my age get to dance with a professional dance troupe? Jill was right. It was the chance of a lifetime. I'd have to be crazy to pass it up.

"Look, I'll make a deal with you," I said. "If you promise not to worry about me, I'll promise to get more rest. Okay?"

She looked at me for a long moment and finally smiled. "Okay, deal. But promise me another thing. Please don't turn into a workaholic like your father. One in the family is enough! In fact, the way you two are going, I'll have to get a career myself, just to keep up."

"Do you ever wish you had stayed in acting?" I asked, suddenly curious. Mom had studied acting in New York after she finished a four-year degree in drama at a university. "Don't you ever miss it?"

The room was very still. "Sometimes," she said finally, twisting a turquoise ring round and round her finger the way she always did when she was bothered by something. "I suppose it was a trade-off. I gave up acting, but look how much I gained. I married your father, and we had you and Daniel."

I personally couldn't see how the Wizard could make up for a brilliant movie career, but I didn't want to make her mad.

"But why couldn't you have done both? Lots of actresses get married and have families too," I said stubbornly.

"Yes, but at that time, it was pretty rare. And I

44

just didn't see how I could combine the two. Acting requires such long hours, such total commitment. In the beginning, your father was just starting his law career, and we had no idea where we would live. By the time I realized we were settled in New York for good, a lot of time had passed. It's hard to say what happened. Things just interfered, I guess."

"What sort of things?"

"Life, mostly. Buying groceries, finding baby-sitters, entertaining your father's clients. Just the day-to-day details of living and taking care of a family. Before I knew what had happened, the years had flown by." She paused, and her eyes looked moist. "Maybe I just wasn't dedicated enough, that's all. Because if I had really felt about acting the way you feel about dancing, I probably wouldn't have let anything stop me."

Her words stayed with me long after she had left the room. I knew one thing for sure. I couldn't let anything stop me! Not even Ian! I resolved to throw myself into my work harder than ever.

I flung open the window and took a deep breath. It was a warm September night, and there was still a hint of honeysuckle in the air. It was a night for walking hand-in-hand, for soft kisses, for tender whispers under the streetlights.

Or for having dinner with Ian at a little candlelit restaurant. The image floated across my mind before I could stop it.

I immediately slammed the window shut and got back to work.

# Chapter 5

I was doing my warm-ups the next morning when the Wizard pounded on my door.

"You're not going to believe it," he said, as if preparing me for a shock, "but a person of the opposite sex is calling you. The same one who called the other night," he added.

*Ian!* I thought and raced down the stairs and snatched the phone.

"Hello," I said breathlessly.

"The pasta wasn't the same without you." I felt a foolish rush of excitement bubble through me. "Was it a nice party?" I asked, not because I really wanted to know, but because I couldn't think of anything else to say.

"It was okay," he said. "Some of the morning show talent came, and Adrienne loved it. She's on a celebrity kick at the moment."

"Adrienne?" I pictured someone blond and beautiful cuddling up to Ian.

"The birthday girl."

"Oh, I thought maybe she was your date," I said foolishly.

He laughed. "No, I had to go alone and heartbroken because you turned me down."

"Well, did you stay late?" I was beginning to sound like his mother.

"Oh, the party lasted until nine, I guess, and then Adrienne invited me back to her apartment for birthday cake."

I hated Adrienne.

I was trying to think of something witty to say when my mom shouted to me from the kitchen. "Your eggs are ready, Kerry."

"Just a minute. I'll be right there," I hissed, putting my hand over the phone.

"I think I caught you at a bad time," Ian said apologetically.

"No, that's okay. Was there anything special . . ."

"Oh," he said casually. "I just wanted to make sure you were taking the train into the city today. There's something I want to ask you."

"You can ask me now," I suggested.

"No, on the phone, my powers are limited. In person, I'm irresistible," he teased me. "I'll see you on the train. Bye, Kerry," he said abruptly and hung up.

I wandered out to the kitchen where Mom greeted me with a platter of bacon and eggs.

"Your friend's an early bird, isn't he?" she asked.

"He has to be if he wants to catch the worm," the Wizard said. "That's you, Kerry!" he yelled, and started laughing so hard you'd think he'd just made the funniest joke in the world.

Someday I'm going to ask a psychiatrist to explain to me how someone with an IQ of 180 can crack up at such stupid jokes. Mom insists that the Wizard will turn into a terrific adult, but I don't know if I can wait that long.

"Is there something special going on today? I ironed your favorite jeans, if you want to wear them. And that new lacy white blouse."

"Thanks," I said, wolfing down my breakfast as fast as I could.

"What's your rush?" She stared at me in surprise. I'm not a morning person, and usually I linger over breakfast as long as I can.

"Just a little studying to do," I shouted as I raced back up to my room. Usually I wear my hair natural, but today I felt like doing something a little extra. I plugged in the hot curlers and tried a bit of mascara and blue eye shadow. While I waited for the little dots on the curlers to change from red to black, I experimented with different smiles in the mirror. I tried a friendly smile, a mysterious smile, and finally the "come-and-get-it" smile that made Shirley Markham so popular. It was no use. No matter how hard I tried, I still looked like me—nice and ordinary.

My classes seemed longer than usual, and I had to use every second of break time to try to finish my assignments. I spent study hall in the library, lost track of the time, and was about fifteen seconds late for French class.

It was a terrible mistake.

Madame Laurent, my French teacher, was a thin, angular woman who never missed a move that anyone made. I tried to slip past her as she was closing the door, but she was too quick for me.

"*Attendez un moment, mademoiselle,*" she said

sharply. *"Vous êtes en retard."* The first time I heard her say that to someone I thought she was telling them they were retarded, but actually, it's just French for "you're late." Punishment was swift: conjugate twenty verbs for every five minutes of tardiness.

"But I was in the library," I started to explain.

*"Vous êtes en retard."*

"Yes, but—"

*"En retard,"* she said coldly, and handed me a mimeographed list of verbs.

At least that was the last period of the day, and nothing worse happened. After school I was so excited about seeing Ian that I ran all the way to the train station.

As I entered "our" car on the train, my eyes started searching immediately for Ian. I saw him grinning and waving at me from the back of the car, and I raced down the aisle. As I settled in next to him, he turned and gave me an appreciative look. "You look fantastic," he said. "Maybe I should sit across from you and enjoy the view. No, I think I'll stay right where I am," he said, putting his arm on top of my seat and then letting it drop casually onto my shoulder. "I want to apologize for being such a turkey yesterday. I've got no right to tell you how to run your life. I've got a bad habit of telling people what to do. But only people I like," he added.

"You don't have to apologize, Ian," I said. "I guess my schedule does seem pretty weird to someone who isn't a dancer. It's just that dancing takes such a huge chunk out of my life, there isn't much time left for anything else."

"I know," he said, "and I swear I'm not going to

pressure you anymore." He paused. "But I am going to make one last offer, Kerry. And it's an offer you can't refuse!"

His laughter was contagious. "Okay, I'll bite. What is it?"

"A bunch of my friends are going to the Horror Movie Marathon at the Kenway Drive-In." He moved a little closer to me. "It's six solid hours of the best horror flicks of all time."

"And you want me to go with you?"

"I insist. In fact, I've already told everyone you're coming," he said.

"I haven't seen a horror movie in years."

"Unbelievable," he said, shaking his head sadly. "You've got a real treat in store for you. *Invasion of the Mushroom People* and *Attack of the Killer Tomatoes* are my all-time favorites."

I had to laugh in spite of myself. "Are those titles for real?"

"And wait till you see *Billy the Kid Versus Dracula*. Now don't tell me you're going to pass up an evening of cultural entertainment like that."

I thought of the resolutions I had made the night before, but it was awfully hard to be practical when Ian was sitting just a couple of inches away.

"There's only one problem, Kerry," Ian said next.

He was rubbing his fingers absentmindedly over my bare shoulder, making a current of electricity dart down my fingertips.

"What's that?" I asked dreamily. For a moment, all my problems had seemed to vanish. But not for long.

"The marathon's tonight," Ian finally blurted out.

"Tonight? But I told you I can't . . . and besides, I'm supposed to audition for *Swan Lake* tonight."

Ian flashed me a sad look with those incredible eyes. "Please, Kerry, can't you audition another night? This really means a lot to me, and I promised my friends I'd bring you. Besides, this is the third time I asked you out. I can't wait forever."

I swallowed hard. Maybe I could work something out. I had to!

"Okay, I'll go. I can audition another night." I spoke quickly before I had a chance to change my mind.

"Good." He gave a sigh of relief. "I knew you'd go."

"You mean you're that sure of your charm?" He knew I was kidding because I was smiling.

"No," he answered. "It's just that I know how much you want to see *The Invasion of the Mushroom People*."

"Well, I'll see you in three hours," I said, turning to leave.

"Wait a minute. I forgot something," he said, holding my elbow.

"What's that?"

To my amazement, he bent down and kissed me lightly on the lips.

"That." He gave me a big smile. "Bye, Kerry."

I still felt warm from his kiss when I got to the studio. The dressing room was throbbing with energy, as dancers peeled off their street clothes and pulled on leotards, tights, and leg-warmers.

Jill was struggling with her "instant warm-up" pants, which have to be the least glamorous clothes ever invented. Lots of nondancers copy our leotards and soft ballet shoes, but no one but a true dancer would ever wear the heavy rubberized pants that Jill had on. They were designed for one use only—to keep the muscles warm and protected during exercise. They're great if you haven't had time to do all the stretches and bends you should do before class, and they're supposed to cut down on injuries. The only trouble is that they make you look like you're wearing an air mattress.

"Tonight's the night," she said in her lilting voice. When I looked blank, she went on cheerfully, "Your audition. And you're going to get a part. I just know it." She slipped an "I Love New York" T-shirt over her head and pulled on a pair of battered ballet shoes.

"Oh, there's been a little change, Jill. I won't be able to audition tonight."

"What?" She started to run a brush through her hair and then stopped to stare at me.

"Something has come up," I said, trying to sound as casual as I could. "I'm going to audition on Monday night instead."

"But you should go tonight," she insisted. "All the good parts may be gone by Monday." She swung her long leg thoughtfully over the chair and took a swig from a diet drink. "Do you have an injury or something?"

"No, I'm fine."

"Then why—"

She was cut off in midsentence by Miss Lili who clapped her hands imperatively. "Girls! Class begins now!"

"I'll explain later," I promised Jill. I smiled to

reassure her, but the truth was that I was baffled too. Choosing a date over an audition was frivolous, irresponsible, and totally out of character.

Then why was I doing it?

I thought of Ian and smiled.

# Chapter 6

"Comfortable?" Ian asked.

We were nestled side by side in Danny deFer-engo's reconditioned 1968 van. My arm, which was pinned against the knotty-pine, paneled wall, was falling asleep. But I wouldn't have moved for the world.

"I'm fine," I said. I was more than fine. I was deliriously happy and had felt that way ever since we boarded the Bronxville train together.

"She should be fine," Danny insisted. "The Yellow Submarine has all the comforts of home."

"It's better than home. It doesn't come with four younger brothers," Sheila said with a laugh.

"It's like an apartment on wheels," he said proudly.

He ran his hand lovingly over the gleaming wooden bar. "Custom paneling all the way," he sighed. "AM-FM stereo, eight-track tape deck, V-8 engine and an overhead console completely covered in genuine cowhide."

I glanced around. The console had enough buttons and gauges to pilot a Boeing 707, and the decor was pure country. There was a tiny rough-hewn table with two barrel chairs, a braided rug, and gingham curtains in the windows. Danny was right. It was like a little apartment on wheels.

"Did it come like this?" I asked.

"No, every bit of it is customized," Shelia said.

"It must have taken months of work."

"Ten, to be exact," she said, and rolled her eyes. "We worked on it every single Saturday. When Danny first bought it, it had been completely stripped. He rebuilt the engine, and I decorated the insides. I put up the panelling, made the curtains, the works."

"You did a fantastic job," I told her, and she smiled at me. She was a thin, pretty girl with gentle blue eyes. I liked her right away.

"The fridge is the best part of the whole deal," Freddie said, handing out Cokes. "If Danny would only get a stove, we could make our own pizzas."

"No way. Nothing can beat Gino's," Lisa said. She was a tall redhead with a terrific figure. She opened up a giant cardboard box and began handing out slices of steaming pizza. We had originally planned on taking the pizza with us to the drive-in, but the smell had been so tantalizing, we decided to eat it right on the spot. We were still parked right in front of Gino's.

I felt a little stab of guilt when the hot cheese and ice-cold Coke hit my mouth. Miss Beatrice believes that dancers "should live on broiled flounder alone," but I excused myself by remembering that this was a special occasion. My first date with Ian! The first of many, I hoped.

"So what do you think of it?" Danny asked, fishing for a compliment. His eyes swept the polished interior of the van.

"It's beautiful," I answered honestly. "I've never been inside a van before."

All five of them stopped eating to stare at me.

"Kerry's a dancer," Ian said, as if that explained everything. I suppose, in a way, it did.

"Really?" Sheila and Lisa said in unison. They looked at me in admiration.

"Do you take lessons from Miss Henrietta?" Lisa asked.

I had to swallow hard. Miss Henrietta is a very sweet old lady who teaches tap dancing to pre-schoolers in a church basement.

"Kerry studies dance in New York," Ian volunteered. You could hear the unmistakable note of pride in his voice.

"I wouldn't mind doing that," Lisa said thoughtfully. "It would be a great excuse to go into the city every Saturday and hit Bloomingdale's. Do you go in once a week?"

"I take class five or six times a week. For three hours."

"Wow! You must be serious about it," Sheila said.

"Is this going to be your career or something?" Lisa asked, handing out seconds on the pizza.

"It's my life," I said simply.

"Heavy," she replied. "I can't imagine practicing anything for three hours a day. I love to disco, though." She paused. "Hey, why don't we all go over to P. J.'s some night next week. You can show me that new step, Ian."

I stared at her and felt a wave of jealousy. If anybody was going to dance with Ian, I wanted it to be me!

"Sure," he said lightly. He reached over and squeezed my hand, which made me feel a lot better.

Then Ian, Danny, and Freddie got into a discussion about five-speed drive transmissions and overhead cam powerplants. The other girls and I smiled nervously at each other, and I tried to think of something to say. I liked them, but I could tell we didn't have much in common. Then Sheila started asking me about some kids from Bronxville that she knew. Once the silence was broken, I relaxed again and started to enjoy myself.

"Anybody want anything else from Gino's before we shove off?" Danny asked. "The first show starts in twenty minutes."

"Let's get a half-gallon of spumoni to go," Sheila said. "I've got some plastic cups and spoons," she said, reaching inside a small cupboard. "Wait till you taste their spumoni, Kerry. It's fantastic!"

"I'll spring for it," Ian said, pulling me to my feet. "C'mon with me, Kerry."

Ian slipped his arm around my waist as soon as we stepped out into the lazy twilight. "Everything okay?" he murmured, giving me a little kiss near my ear.

"Everything's . . . fabulous." I know that some of the advice columns tell you to play it cool around boys, but I just couldn't hide the fact that I was having a wonderful time.

"For me, too." He smiled at me and held the door open to Gino's. It was dark and inviting, with red-checked tablecloths and glowing candles. I found myself wishing the two of us were spending the evening there alone, and he smiled down at me, as if he were reading my mind.

"We'll come here for dinner soon, okay?"

Soon! I didn't let myself worry about how I'd fit it into my schedule. I knew I wanted to see Ian again.

"I was afraid maybe you were getting bored with all that talk about the van," he said. "Danny's a nice guy, but he gets a little carried away with his pride and joy."

"No, that's okay. Your friends are really great, Ian. Usually I find it hard to talk to people who aren't dancers."

"Except for me, I hope."

"You're an exception to every rule."

It was true. Ian was one of the few nondancers I felt comfortable with. Dancers just seem to have a built-in code that makes words unnecessary. It's like ESP or something. Who else but another dancer could understand the bone-weary pain after hours of practice, the thrill of a perfect *tour en l'air*, the numbing agony of shin splints? You just can't communicate those feelings to someone who isn't a dancer. You have to experience them for yourself to know what they're really like.

It was barely dark when we got to the drive-in, but dozens of cars were tooting their horns, impatient for the first feature to begin.

The van seemed roomier once we rearranged ourselves. Danny and Sheila sat in the bucket swivel seats up front, Lisa and Freddie perched on the narrow, bunk-style bed, and Ian and I shared a barrel chair.

"You sure you're not packed in like sardines back there?" Danny yelled.

"Of course we are, but who cares? We're all friends!" Lisa answered.

"We may not be after being cooped up in here for six hours," Sheila teased.

Six hours! My mind stopped short. When I had telephoned home and told mom I was going to the movie with Ian, I had said I'd be home at midnight.

"This lasts six hours?" I said weakly to Ian.

"Sure, I told you that on the train. Why?"

I kept my voice low so his friends wouldn't hear. "Look, I don't want to sound like Cinderella, but I've never been out past midnight."

"Really?"

I seemed to be surprising everyone tonight.

"Well, maybe you should call your mother again. There's a phone at the food stand."

"Ian, it's not just my mother I'm worried about. I can't stay out that late, or I'll be a wreck tomorrow." I thought of the piles of research notes lying untouched on my desk.

"Oh," he said, disappointed. Then his smile came back. "Aren't you forgetting something? Tomorrow's Saturday. You can sleep late."

"Afraid not," I muttered, as a crackle of static announced the first movie.

"A frenzy of blood," the announcer was saying in a stagey voice. A monster weaved across the screen as the sound track built to a deafening crescendo. "Haunting desires seething in his brain lead to a night of ghastly terrors!" On closer inspection, you could see that the monster was really a man wrapped in yards of gauze bandages. The man-monster stumbled around for a while, bumping into trees and bushes in an out-of-focus forest.

I giggled in spite of myself, then tugged at Ian's sleeve impatiently. "Ian, what am I going to do?"

"About what?" He was watching the screen, transfixed.

"Ian, I can't stay for the whole six hours," I said desperately.

He turned to me and blinked, like a man coming out of a trance.

"I have to be in New York at nine tomorrow morning. I can't sleep late, like you said."

Comprehension finally dawned on him. "You have classes on Saturday mornings?"

"Sometimes," I admitted. "If we don't get through all of the routines, Miss Beatrice usually calls another class over the weekend."

"Wow," he said quietly. "Let me figure something out." He paused and thought for a moment. "It will be okay," he said finally. "Everybody always gets bored by the second feature anyway, so they'll probably be ready to leave before midnight." When I didn't say anything, he added, "I'll make sure you get home on time, Kerry. I promise. Now relax and enjoy the movie."

"All right. Thanks." I smiled at him gratefully. I didn't want to be a drag, but I didn't want to spend Saturday morning bumbling through class, either.

When I looked at the screen again, the monster had changed into a werewolf, but no one in the van seemed confused by the abrupt plot change. Ian grabbed my hand and said excitedly, "This is the best part, Kerry. You've never seen anything like it!"

That much was true. The werewolf was wearing a white lab coat. He had either developed a sudden interest in research, or he was changing into a mad scientist. Or maybe he was changing back into a mad scientist. It was impossible to tell.

He was holding a test tube up to the light, examining a strange-looking potion. He looked as though he had just made a major breakthrough, like inventing Alka-Seltzer. The camera zoomed in for a close-up, and we were treated to the sight of his yellowing fangs breaking into a wide grin.

"He looks like Mr. Petri," Danny howled. "He's our new lab assistant," he explained for my benefit.

"No, Mr. Petri has more hair on his face," Ian said.

I never could figure out the plot, but it didn't matter, because Sheila and Lisa kept up a running commentary on the action on the screen. The whole thing was perfectly silly, and I loved it.

Ian was sitting as close to me as was humanly possible and was running his hand up and down my arm. I had never felt so wonderful. I snuggled close and smiled at him.

We had moved on to *The Invasion of the Mushroom People*, and Lisa buried her head in Freddie's shoulder every time one of the giant fungi appeared on the screen.

This plot was even more complicated, although it seemed to involve a group of Japanese voyagers who drift off-course and end up on a deserted island. Deserted except for a species of giant mushrooms, naturally. We watched the deadly fungi consume everything in their path, and I swore I'd never eat another stuffed mushroom. I was trying not to yawn, when the film broke in the middle.

There was a loud wail from Danny. "Oh, no! Right at the best part!"

"Maybe they'll put on something else," Sheila said, trying to look on the bright side.

"There aren't many movies like that one," Danny said sadly.

"That's certainly true," I whispered to Ian, and he rewarded me with a broad smile.

"Want some popcorn?" He gave my hand a little squeeze.

Throwing caution to the wind, I said, "Sure. With butter."

"Anyone else want anything?"

"No, we're fine." There was a chorus of giggles from the darkened van.

The air was cool and sweet, and I took a deep breath. Ian held my hand lightly as we walked to the concession stand.

"I'm having a great time," he said in a husky voice.

"Even without *The Invasion of the Mushroom People*?"

"I'll survive. *Attack of the Killer Tomatoes* is on next, anyway."

"I can hardly wait," I said, grinning at him.

"Yeah, I still can't believe you've never heard of it. You must have been living in a cave all these years. Sometime you've got to tell me what you do for recreation."

"I've already told you."

"I know. *Pliés, relevés, chassés, battements tendus* . . ."

I stared at him in astonishment. "How do you know all that?"

"I told you I'm a trivia buff. I'm working my way through a dance encyclopedia, page by page."

"You're learning about ballet just for me?"

"Of course. I'll learn about ballet, and you'll learn about horror movies." He pulled me into the shadows near the popcorn stand. "And other things," he whispered, wrapping his arms around me.

"What was your favorite?" Ian asked, as we sat close together on the ride home. Just as he had predicted, everyone was ready to leave at eleven thirty.

I thought for a minute. "*Attack of the Killer Tomatoes*, I guess."

"I told you it was a classic," he replied happily. "I knew it would have an effect on you."

He was right. Nothing had prepared me for the rampaging tomatoes. Slurping and gurgling, they had pulverized everything in sight, until they were herded into a San Diego football stadium where they miraculously shrunk to normal size.

"The song was really unique," I said thoughtfully.

"You mean, 'I know I'm going to miss her, a tomato ate my sister'? That's one of my favorites, too."

"I thought it would be," I said, trying to keep a straight face.

He had just leaned over to kiss me, when we pulled up in front of my house.

"Sure you don't want to come to Denny's with us?" Sheila asked.

"Sorry, I've got an early class tomorrow," I said quickly. I thought Ian might kiss me at the door, but we both were aware of four pairs of eyes trying not to watch us from the van.

"I really enjoyed it, Ian. Thanks a lot."

"It's just the beginning, Kerry. I'll call you tomorrow."

"Make it in the afternoon, okay? I don't know how long I'll be tied up at the studio."

He gave me a light peck on the cheek, and it was all I could do to keep from wrapping my arms around his neck. The porch light snapped on, stifling any impulse I might have had, so I contented myself with a whispered 'Bye.' "

"How was your evening, honey?" my mother asked half a minute later. She and the Wizard were watching the late show on TV.

"Interesting."

She knows that whenever I say something is interesting, it means that I haven't really sorted out my impressions.

"She means the jury is still out," the Wizard couldn't resist saying. It was kind of a family joke.

Mom smiled, but didn't press me for details. "So you found out that you liked horror movies after all?"

"Oh, yes," I said seriously. "As an art form, they offer . . . quite a bit more than I expected."

I gave her a quick wink, over the Wizard's head, and darted up to my room.

# Chapter 7

Flex, Point. Stretch. Release. My leg was raised in a quivering *développé* to just below waist level. I gritted my teeth and tried to extend it another couple of inches, but it just hung there quivering.

We had been practicing for two hours, and every nerve ending in my body was on fire. It was thirty minutes past break time, but no one had the nerve to tell Miss Beatrice.

I glanced at Jill and saw that she, too, was showing the strain. Her face was pale and shiny with perspiration, and her lower lip had almost disappeared as her mouth contorted in a tight line.

In spite of her weariness and pain, though, her technique was still perfect. Her back was ramrod straight, her head and neck in perfect alignment. Her neck arched forward gracefully to follow the movement of her arm, as if she were reaching toward an invisible goal.

"The leg should make a ninety-degree angle with the body," Miss Beatrice announced, moving along the line of dancers. At times like these, she reminded me of a giant sea bird skimming the room for prey; she had an uncanny ability to spot the weak, the timid, the careless.

"Don't tell me you can't do it. Show me you can," she insisted. She was tapping her yardstick rhythmically on the polished floor when she stopped suddenly and stared at me. "Higher, Kerry."

I tried to force the leg to the ideal ninety-degree angle, but it rebelled. It felt as heavy and lifeless as a statue's, and it was taking every ounce of my concentration just to hold it there.

"I don't think—"

"Don't think. Just do." The dancer's creed. No apologies, no complaints. I had been trained to obey orders for the past nine years, and I automatically struggled to obey now.

I took a deep breath and tightened my aching stomach muscles. *Lift. Lift.* Miraculously, the leg lifted higher in the air, as if it were being pulled by invisible strings. It was shaking furiously, but it was now at a ninety-degree angle to my body.

I watched it, mesmerized, as hot tears stung my eyes and threatened to pour down my cheeks. It seemed strangely disembodied, as if it belonged to someone else.

I held the position, trembling, waiting for a word from Miss Beatrice. "It hurts," I muttered between clenched teeth.

"Yes," she said calmly, "it's supposed to."

After what seemed like forever, she turned away and clapped her hands sharply. "Change sides!"

There was a collective groan as the struggle began again. And again. I had just as much trouble on this side, but I was determined not to let Miss Beatrice pounce on me again.

Lift it steadily. Don't think. Ignore the pain. Or if you can't ignore it, work through it. Every breath was a painful rattle now, and I felt as if my lungs were going to explode.

Miss Beatrice was working her way toward me again, and I felt a terrible panic in the pit of my stomach. With an almost superhuman effort, I raised my leg waist-high and forced it to stay there. Every muscle was alive and throbbing, but the leg remained in position. I blocked out the noise and the music, closing my eyes against the red mist of pain that rose inside me.

I bit my lip and tasted blood.

Just when I thought I couldn't hold on for another second, Miss Beatrice appeared at my side, fixing me with a bright, hard look. I never knew what to expect from her—a command, a warning, a reproach, a tongue-lashing.

This time she surprised me. "Take a break, everyone," she said softly. She was very close to me, and just for a moment, I thought I saw a flicker of sympathy in those hard green eyes.

"Sometimes I think we're all insane," Jill said. She had thrown a towel around her shoulders and was sprawled in a bean-bag chair in the corner of the studio.

"All dancers are insane," Abby said. Long-legged, long-necked, lean bodied, Abby was the oldest member of the class, a veteran performer at nineteen.

"Are you two doing *Swan Lake*?" she asked us.

A tired smile lit up Jill's face. "I sure am!"

"How about you, Kerry?"

"Uh . . . probably."

"Probably!" Jill was stunned. "You just told me you're going to audition on Monday night."

I was about to explain when Abby cut in smoothly.

"Monday's your last chance, you know. Mr. Rudikoff plans on having everything cast by then, because there's hardly any time for rehearsal. It's going to be one of his usual rush jobs."

"Have you worked with him before?" Jill asked.

"Oh, sure," Abby replied. "And believe me, it's worth the effort. He demands a lot from his dancers, but he's a fantastic teacher. You learn more in one of his rehearsals than you do in a dozen classes. But don't tell Miss Beatrice I said that." She smiled and moved back to the barre, and I watched her, fascinated.

She did a series of deep *pliés*, and then went into an amazing *arabesque.* Her slender chest was thrust forward, and her long red hair streamed out behind her. She could have been a figurehead on a nineteenth-century ship.

"I think she does barre work in her sleep," Jill muttered. "She exercises every waking moment. You'd think just once she'd feel like collapsing like the rest of us!" She paused and turned to me. "What's this about you not going to the audition?"

"I said I'd *probably* go," I countered.

"Probably!" she exploded. "You have a chance to appear with Natalie Petrov and work with a director like Mr. Rudikoff, and you say you'll *probably* go? Are you sure you haven't fallen on your head?"

"It's a long story." I tried to get comfortable on a metal folding chair, gave up, and dropped to the floor. I shoved my towel under my head for a pillow and closed my eyes.

"Don't go to sleep," she threatened. "I want an answer."

"All right, I'll go. Definitely."

"Well, I should hope so," she said, relieved. "For a moment, I thought you had lost your mind."

Just my heart, I felt like saying.

She took a long drink from her diet soda, and then pressed the icy can against her flushed cheeks and forehead. "This was a killer of a class," she sighed. "I was okay until those *arabesques*, and then everything—"

"Jill," I interrupted suddenly, "what did you do last night?"

"What I always do." She looked surprised at the question. "Dinner. Then homework. Then practice." She stretched her foot out and examined it for bumps and ridges. She ran her fingers over it coolly and clinically, as if it were an archaelogical find. "How about you?" she asked, staring at me.

"I had a wonderful time," I said slowly. I raised my arms over my head in an enormous stretch and felt all the tension ease out of the overworked muscles and ligaments. I lay back on the floor, limp and relaxed. "I went to a horror movie marathon."

"Now I know you've lost your mind."

"No, you don't understand. It was a date."

"A date?" she sniffed suspiciously.

"Right," I agreed happily. "In a van."

"I don't believe this."

I flopped over on my stomach and rested my chin

in my hands. "There were a lot of 'firsts' last night," I babbled on, in spite of her disapproving look. "The first time in a van, the first time at a drive-in movie, the first horror movie marathon I've ever seen—"

"I hope there weren't too many firsts," she said pointedly.

"No, of course not," I said, feeling my cheeks get scarlet. "Nothing like that. Just a friendly kiss. Oh, Jill, I had such a great time. No one was a dancer—" I stopped as a dark look crossed her face. "Wait, I didn't mean that the way it sounded. I meant they were just ordinary people—Civilians."

She didn't answer. I glanced at her, but her profile was so calm and controlled, it was impossible to guess what she was thinking.

"You see, I met this really neat boy named Ian on the train. He kept asking me out, and I kept refusing, and then he asked me to this movie marathon."

"And you weakened."

"No, not weakened. I guess I just realized how much I liked him and how much I really wanted to go out with him. It just sounded like so much fun. *He's* so much fun. One of his friends, Danny, has this crazy, reconditioned van, and a bunch of us went to the Kenway Drive-In. We stopped for pizza at Gino's, and there's this little refrigerator in the van. Danny keeps it stocked with Cokes and snacks . . ."

"And *that's* why you missed the audition," she said in a thin voice.

"Yes," I said. Why couldn't she, of all people, understand? I sat up and faced her. "Jill," I said slowly, "do you know how long it's been since I've had a day off, or even a night off? Do you know how long it's been since I've really had any fun or had time to do anything crazy?"

"I know you missed an important audition," she said coolly, looking away from me.

I could tell I wasn't making any headway with her. She stood up and tugged at her leg-warmers, which were bunched up around her ankles.

"I hope you know what you're doing, Kerry," she said over her shoulder. She was already on her way back to the barre.

"Wait a minute."

I scrambled to my feet, but we never had a chance to finish our discussion. In a moment, Miss Beatrice reappeared, signaled to the piano player, and class began again.

"Have time for lunch?" Jill asked me. She gave a tentative little smile, and I knew she wanted to smooth things over between us.

"I think I'm broke," I said, rummaging in my duffel bag.

"I meant at my house, silly! I don't think my mother will charge you for a grilled cheese sandwich," she said, laughing.

"Then I accept. In fact, I may even ask for seconds," I added, as my stomach rumbled warningly. I had dashed out of the house without breakfast that morning, and I was feeling lightheaded.

We were almost out the door when we were stopped by a firm command from Miss Beatrice. "Can I see both of you for a minute?" It sounded like a question, but we both knew what it really was: a royal command.

"Of course," I gulped nervously. "What's up?" I mouthed at Jill as we headed back to Miss Beatrice's cluttered little office.

"Beats me," Jill muttered. "I just hope it doesn't take long."

"Sit down, girls," our teacher said warmly.

Jill took the chair opposite the battered desk, and I looked warily around the room.

"There. There," Miss Beatrice said, pointing to a canvas director's chair that was littered with ballet books. Her tone was impatient, but she was smiling. I was confused by the mixed signals and looked questioningly at Jill. It was obvious that she was baffled too.

I put the books carefully on the floor and waited for Miss Beatrice to begin.

"The door. Shut the door." She waited until Jill obeyed and then said, "Some of the other girls are still here, and I want this to be a private conversation." Her voice was still friendly, and I was more puzzled than ever.

"If it's about that *développé*," I began hesitantly.

"No, no," she said, dismissing the idea with a wave. "I'm not worried about your *développés*. You and Jill are both very talented young dancers. Naturally, you both have rough spots that need attention, but nothing that a lot of hard work can't cure. All in all, I'm very happy with your progress."

I looked at Jill in amazement. Coming from Miss Beatrice, this was high praise. There was a running gag at the studio that if Miss Beatrice ever met Margot Fonteyn, the world-famous ballerina,

72

she would probably tell her that her work was "adequate."

Jill looked as if the suspense was killing her. She was perched on the edge of the chair, with two pinpoints of color in her cheeks. She looked like she was holding her breath.

Miss Beatrice pulled an envelope out of nowhere, like a stage magician doing a trick. I noticed that it was plastered with foreign stamps.

"From Paris," Miss Beatrice said mysteriously.

Jill forgot to be terrified and let out a whoop of excitement. "It's from L'Étoile, right? I can't believe it!" She tore into the letter, but in her excitement, she dropped it on the floor and had to search around under the desk for it.

She banged her head lightly coming back up, but seemed not to notice. "I hope it's in English," she said suddenly.

"It is," Miss Beatrice assured her. "Now don't get too excited yet. It's only the preliminary application, but as you can see, you're definitely in the running."

"Oh, I'm shaking too much to read it, Miss Beatrice. Just tell me what it says."

She turned to me as if she had just remembered that I was there. "Kerry," she said breathlessly, "do you remember when I told you I was applying for a scholarship to study in France? This is it."

Miss Beatrice scanned the letter and handed it back to her. "You've made it over the first hurdle, Jill. They want some more information about you, and some additional references from your teachers. Also, they say that you sound like a remarkable young woman, and they wish you the best of luck."

"Jill, that's fantastic. If anyone deserves a scholarship, it's you." I was thrilled for her. All the long years of practice had finally paid off.

"There's more," Miss Beatrice said in a low voice. She looked at both of us. "I'm sharing this news with you for a special reason, Kerry. Not just because you're Jill's friend. L'Étoile has asked me to recommend another student to them, and I was going to suggest you."

"Apply for a scholarship to Paris?" I stammered.

"Of course!" Jill shrieked in my ear. "It's perfect! Why didn't I think of it? We'll be roommates in France. Just think of it!"

I was still too stunned to speak, but Jill steadied herself and said to Miss Beatrice, "What does she have to do?"

"There's an extra set of forms here for her," Miss Beatrice said. "She'll have to have her parents sign them and return them to me, and then I'll add a letter of recommendation." She was speaking about me as if I weren't even in the room.

"And of course, I'll help you any way I can," she said, turning to me with a big smile. "Be sure to tell your parents that they can call me any time if they would like to talk it over. I know it's a big decision for them to make. But I do think it's the right one, or I never would have suggested it. You and Jill both have the talent and the determination . . . You'd both make the most of the experience." She stood up and threw a battered raincoat over her practice clothes. "You'll have to excuse me now, girls. I have another rehearsal clear across town, and have just"—she glanced at her watch—"twenty minutes to get there."

"Of course, Miss Beatrice," Jill said. Even in moments of crisis, she never forgot her manners. She pulled me to my feet. My legs were wooden and refused to move, like a stubborn puppet's.

"I'll take these right home to my mother," she said, clutching the fat envelope to her side.

Scholarship? L'Étoile? Paris? A million questions raced through my mind, but I couldn't formulate them. It wasn't until we were standing outside the studio that I realized that I hadn't even thanked Miss Beatrice.

Lunch at Jill's turned out to be a three-hour celebration. Mrs. Abbott insisted on making a huge brunch of honey-dipped French toast, sizzling bacon and sausage links, and a pyramid of scrambled eggs.

"What a shame your mother isn't here with us," she said to me. "We'll have to do this again whenever she can come into the city. After all," she said with a smile, "we have a lot in common now." She was obviously taking it for granted that Jill and I would both be accepted and would go to Paris together.

Jill was too excited to eat and was happily poring over the brochures. "Listen to this, Kerry. The school arranges sightseeing tours for the foreign students. They have picnics on the Seine, and they visit Versailles and the chateâu in the Loire Valley . . . and look, here's a picture of them strolling through the Left Bank. And Montmartre, the student district. Oh, this is too good to be true. It really is!"

"If you read me anything else out of that catalog, I'm going to run away to Paris myself," Mrs. Abbott teased her. "Now have some breakfast," she insisted. "Before you know it, you'll be living on coffee and croissants."

"And listen to this!" Jill said without looking up. "You get every Friday afternoon off! That does it, Kerry. You and I have got to go."

"What about school?" I asked her.

"Well, it says right here that you spend mornings at the American Institute taking high school courses, and then you go to L'Étoile in the afternoon. All your time is organized; it's all part of the same program."

"That's one of the things that really appealed to me," Mrs. Abbott said. "I don't know about you, Kerry, but Jill always seems to be racing from one thing to another, spinning her wheels. I think she could accomplish more in a program that combined schoolwork and dance."

"Do you have to speak French? I can't speak it very well."

"I hope not," Jill giggled. "No, it says that all the classes at the American Institute are in English. And we know enough French to get through the dance classes." She was right. It doesn't matter where you are in the world, dance is taught in one language—French.

"You're really planning on going, aren't you?"

"Of course. If I'm accepted." She studied the forms for a moment. "You'll have to fill these out right away, Kerry, because the deadline is coming up soon. In fact, if we're accepted, we have to leave in six weeks."

"Six weeks!"

"That's right. The next session starts on November 15, so there's no time to waste."

"And how long . . . would we stay there?" I said weakly.

"Until the end of the school year in May!"

"It sounds overwhelming."

"No, it isn't. Just think how exciting it will be to live in Paris—the most romantic city in the world. We'll be sharing a room together in a pension. That's like a French boardinghouse," she explained. "Oh, Kerry, we're going to have such a wonderful time! Living in Paris! It's absolutely perfect."

Not quite, I thought. It sounded exciting, but it also sounded scary and more than a little lonely. Not only would I miss my parents—and even the Wizard—but I'd probably never see Ian again.

"Let me know what your folks say. You don't know how happy I am that you're coming with me. We're going to get along great together. How could we miss?" she said with a laugh. "After all, we're both dancers. We want exactly the same things."

I wondered whether she was right.

# Chapter 8

"Hi." Ian's voice was warm and sexy on the phone.

"Ian," I said, delighted. "I just got in the door. You must have ESP."

"Of course," he said. "Our spirits are so much in tune that I'm aware of all your movements. I know everything about you."

"Then tell me what I'm wearing right this minute."

"That's easy." He paused. "Something soft and flowing. Light blue, I think. Very feminine and very pretty. A blouse and skirt."

"Gotcha." I started to giggle.

"What's wrong?"

"Ian, I hate to disillusion you, but I'm wearing a pair of grimy dark green sweat pants, a bright red top, and a pair of white Adidas."

"Well, nobody's perfect," he said.

"You remind me of one of those would-be psychics who try to predict your astrological sign and always get it wrong."

"I was saving that for tonight."

I had no idea what he was talking about. "Tonight?"

"Our Italian restaurant . . . just like in the Billy Joel song."

Ian's conversation was harder to follow than usual.

"Gino's," he explained when I didn't say anything. "Remember, we made a date to go to Gino's soon. This is soon."

"Tonight?"

"Soon enough."

"Ian," I began and stopped. I really had no idea how to explain to him that I couldn't see him all the time. That I couldn't even see him on regular dates the way other girls could. The terrible part was that I really wanted to.

"Ian, I'm not like other girls you know." It was a bad beginning.

"I know that," he said. "You're beautiful, intelligent, and charming. In fact, you're the perfect date."

"That isn't what I meant." I sighed. "Look, Ian, you've got to understand that I'm a dancer. A dancer," I repeated, hoping it would sink in. "I don't have time to go out with boys much. I barely even see my own family."

"Then we'll take them to Gino's too," he said, refusing to be serious.

"Ian."

"All right," he relented. "Tell me what you have to do tonight that's so pressing. I bet I can figure out a solution."

"I'll bet you can't. I have to write a rough draft of my term paper, which is still sitting in pieces on

79

my desk. I have to do some math problems. I have to study for a French test . . ." The list went on, but I heard Ian sigh, so I cut it short

"You have to eat dinner, don't you?"

"Well, I really should eat dinner with my parents tonight," I hedged. "There's something I need to talk to them about."

"Then I'll see you after dinner. Remember how much you liked that spumoni? We'll go to Gino's for dessert. Cappuccino and spumoni. And I promise to get you home early so you can burn the midnight oil, or whatever it is you do."

I knew that I couldn't refuse him. He was probably counting on that, I told myself. Ian wasn't conceited, but he certainly wasn't unaware of his charm.

"Well, if you don't mind bringing me home by ten."

"Of course not. After all, I know that I'll have you all to myself tomorrow, at Coney Island."

"Coney Island!"

"You've never been there, right?"

"Maybe when I was two years old, but what does that have to do with anything?"

"It's time to go again. See you at seven thirty," he said and hung up.

I put down the receiver and sighed in exasperation. Coney Island! I took a deep breath and looked at my watch. Four o'clock. The TV was silent, so the Wizard was probably out playing with his friends. I heard music coming from the kitchen and decided that this would be a good time to talk to Mom about Paris.

"Hi, honey," she said. "Dinner will be another hour. Are you hungry?"

"No, that's okay. I had a huge brunch at Jill's and I'm stuffed. I really just wanted to talk to you about something."

"Sure." She rinsed her hands at the sink and sat down at the kitchen table. "Is there anything wrong?"

I tried to ignore the fluttery feeling in my chest, and as calmly as I could, I told her about L'Etoile. She listened intently, and her eyes never left my face. When she looked at the brochure, she smiled. "I always wanted to go to Paris," she said softly.

"You did?" There was so much about her that I didn't know.

"And Miss Beatrice is going to recommend you for a scholarship?"

"Yes."

"Congratulations." She broke into a wide grin. "Whether you accept it or not, it's an honor you'll always remember."

I didn't say anything, and she stared at me. "That's the tough part, isn't it? Deciding whether or not to go for it."

I nodded. "I thought you and Dad would have something to say about that." I grinned at her.

"Well, of course your father and I need to talk it over and think about it very seriously. But in the end, it will be your decision, Kerry. If dancing is the most important thing to you, and I think it is, this could be a very important move for your career. Tell me," she said, "what was *your* first reaction?"

I laughed, remembering how Jill had had to

steer me out of Miss Beatrice's office. "First I was stunned, and then I was excited and interested and scared. All at the same time."

"I'm not surprised. Living in a strange country for the next few months would instill a little fear in anyone. But that doesn't mean you shouldn't do it, you know."

The oven buzzer went off, and she stood up. "I'll lay the groundwork with your father, and get his reaction, if you like." She came behind my chair and hugged me. "I know he's going to be very, very proud of you, Kerry." She smiled, and I reminded myself for the zillionth time how great it was to have her always on my side. I knew Mom would support me in whatever I decided to do. But she was right. The tough part was making the decision.

Dad never made it home to dinner after all, so Mom and the Wizard and I took trays into the den and watched the news. As soon as it was over, I dashed upstairs to get ready to meet Ian.

I had just finished showering when I heard Mom greeting him downstairs. On an impulse, I pulled on a light blue blouse and shirt, very soft and feminine, just like in Ian's prediction. It was worth it, when I saw the look on his face.

"Wow!" he said appreciatively.

"Every psychic needs to be right once in a while," I teased him.

"You really do look beautiful," he told me later at Gino's. My spumoni was melting in the dish because Ian was holding my right hand in his, and it was awkward to eat with my left.

"In fact, you look like the perfect Pisces."

"What?"

"The perfect Pisces," he repeated calmly.

"You're trying to guess my sign!"

"I don't have to guess. Now that I've gotten to know you, I see that there's only one sign you could be. Pisces. It's a snap. You're warm, generous, talented, and you're obviously very creative. Most people in creative fields are Pisces, did you know that?"

He edged a little closer to me on the red leather seat, and I forgot about the melting spumoni and the cooling cappuccino. His face was just inches from mine. "And you're smart and have a good sense of humor, two other Pisces traits. You're very loyal to your friends, you love animals, and you're just a tiny bit impatient. Am I right?"

"You are," I admitted. It was amazing. Maybe there was something to astrology after all. "You really figured all this out about me in such a short time?"

"It's all true, isn't it?" he countered. "You are a Pisces?"

"Yes, and I'm really impressed. You *are* psychic."

I looked at him, and he burst out laughing, breaking the spell.

"What's so funny?" I demanded. People at other tables were beginning to stare at him.

"I'm not psychic," he said, when he managed to speak again. I must have looked puzzled because he laughed even harder. "I . . . I bribed your younger brother to tell me your birthday."

Ian kept his promise and got me home at ten,

but I was too tired to accomplish very much on my term paper anyway. I struggled through my index cards, checked some footnotes, and gave up before midnight.

When the alarm went off the next morning, I felt as if someone had fired a cannon in my ear. I sat straight up in bed, shivering. The room was cold, and the flat gray light creeping in the window made it seem earlier than six.

I felt as though I hadn't even gone to bed.

I stumbled downstairs and was surprised to see Dad in the kitchen, surrounded by his law books. I'm sure he's the only person in the world who reads legal briefs for fun.

"What's up? You're not at the office?" I teased him.

"I'm going in late today," he said, giving me a big smile. Dad usually put in some time at the office on Sunday afternoon. "But I couldn't leave until I congratulated the star ballerina."

"Not quite." I grinned at him. I sat down and watched dully as he poured me a cup of coffee. How anyone could function at full steam at six A.M. was beyond me.

"Your mother told me the news. You don't know how proud we are of you, honey." He reached across the table and gave my hand a squeeze.

I took a few sips of the scalding coffee and slowly came back to life. "But what's the verdict?" I said finally.

"You're the jury," he said with a grin.

"But what do you think about it?" I persisted.

"I think it's marvelous!" he said heartily. "I want to talk to Miss Beatrice, of course, and find out more of the details. But there's no harm in going ahead with the application forms. I've already signed them, and you can return them to her tomorrow."

Everything was moving much faster than I had anticipated.

He knew something was wrong, because he stared at me for a long moment. "I guess the jury is still out," he said softly.

"It's just that I don't know if I want to be gone from home all that time," I said in an unsteady voice. "I'd miss all of you so much . . ." I stopped. Even the thought of leaving home brought hot tears to my eyes.

"Kerry, honey," he said, walking around the table to hug me, "we'd miss you, too. Terribly. But November to May isn't as long as you think, and besides, what if the three of us came over there to see you at Easter?"

"I'd love it!" It had never occurred to me that they might be able to visit me. "You really think I should do it, don't you?"

He waited a minute before replying. "If dancing is as important to you as I think it is . . . then yes, Kerry, I really do. But only you can answer that. And believe me, we're not pushing you to go to Paris. We've gotten kind of used to having you around these past fifteen years." He smiled at me, and I felt my eyes water up again.

"I guess you feel about dancing the way I feel about law," he went on. "But you've got the jump on me. I didn't discover law until I was in college, and you've been dancing since you were six." He paused. "We're both very lucky, Kerry," he said seriously. "We both found something in life we love to do."

By eleven thirty, I realized that I had been insane to agree to go to Coney Island with Ian. My research paper was in a shambles, my math equations didn't balance, and my French verbs were as unconjugated as ever.

I realized something else: I wanted to see him again.

"Your friendly tour guide at your service," he said when he picked me up at noon. He looked more handsome than ever in faded jeans and a pale blue cotton shirt.

As we rode the train into the city, Ian planned our trips for the next six months. If I went to even half the places he mentioned, I would have to give up eating and sleeping.

"How do you fit everything in?" I asked him at one point. "You must study sometime."

"Play first, work second. That's my motto," he said, smiling.

"But you can't go through life like that."

"You can't?" he said, in such a pathetic voice that I burst out laughing.

"No, you can't," I answered firmly. "You've got to have goals, plans, ambitions."

"I do. I plan on enjoying myself every minute I'm alive. Admit it, you like to have fun too. It's just that you hardly ever let yourself." He looked me over with those piercing gray eyes and smiled.

"There are different kinds of fun, Ian," I said helplessly. I remembered what my father had said that morning. "I'm lucky to have my dancing. It's something I love—and that I'm good at," I said, a little defensively.

"Oh, you're good at lots of things, take my word for it!" He grinned and kissed me before I could say another word.

When we stepped off the subway at Coney Island, a pale watery sun had just emerged from behind the clouds.

"See, what did I tell you? I knew it was going to be a terrific day!" Ian shouted. His gaze took in the sun glittering on the water, the foamy whitecaps crashing against the shore, the miles of deserted beach. He was delighted with everything, as usual. I looked at his handsome face and strong, muscled body and felt a warm glow go through me. Ian was right: He *did* know how to have a good time.

He flung an arm over my shoulder, and we decided to trek the length of the boardwalk. The sun was warm on our faces, and the salty breeze riffled Ian's dark hair.

"A perfect afternoon," he murmured into my ear.

We stopped for hot dogs and ate them with our feet propped up on a rickety wooden railing. For some reason, they tasted better than anything I had ever eaten in my whole life. When I told Ian, he laughed. "Sure, everybody knows you have to eat hot dogs at the ocean. Just like nothing can beat a pizza at a drive-in," he reminded me. "Or peanuts at the zoo," he said, after a minute. "We'll do that next week."

Next week! I knew I should say something. It was the perfect opportunity. I should tell Ian about my audition for *Swan Lake*, about L'Étoile in Paris, about my chance for a scholarship. I stared at his handsome profile, and the words stuck in my throat. Ian was the most attractive, exciting boy I had ever met. How could I tell him I wouldn't be able to spend much time with him?

After lunch, we took off our shoes and walked along the shore, letting the freezing salt water run over our toes. The temperature had dropped, and the sun was sinking low on the horizon. I must have shivered because he stopped and looked at me.

"Cold?" he asked.

"A little," I admitted.

"Why didn't you say so?" He pulled me against him and gave me a long kiss. Everything seemed to stand still, like a freeze-frame picture, and I knew that the foamy whitecaps, the cry of the gulls, and Ian's warm kiss could be imprinted on my memory forever.

I finally forced myself to pull away. "It's time to get back," I said gently.

He checked his watch. "I hate to say it, but I guess you're right."

We sat curled up next to each other on the train ride home, holding hands, exchanging jokes, happy to be together.

"I can't wait to see you tomorrow," he said. "Twice!"

I knew he meant our roundtrip train ride. But of course I wouldn't be seeing him on the way back because I was auditioning for *Swan Lake* tomorrow after class.

"Ian—" He started to kiss me, and the rest of my words were swallowed up.

"What?" he whispered in a husky voice.

"It's not important," I said. I put my arms around his neck and returned his kiss.

# Chapter 9

The next day was an example of Murphy's Law in action: If something *can* go wrong, it *will* go wrong.

It did. All day long.

I overslept, and in a mad rush to get out of the house, I left my French verbs, neatly conjugated, sitting on the dresser. Madame Laurent stared at me as if I were a criminal, then gave me twenty more to do as a "late penalty." If she hadn't decided to be a teacher, she would have made a brilliant prosecutor.

My chemistry experiment dissolved like limp Kleenex instead of forming cheerful crystals, and I stumbled into Civics just in time for a pop quiz. The fateful words: "Close your books and take out a sheet of paper" rang in my brain like a death knell, and my mind was as blank as the paper.

We exchanged papers to grade them, and when Harry Talbot handed mine back, an evil smirk lit up his freckled face. "Boy, Kerry, you really blew it this time," he said, delighted. He scribbled an enormous D on the paper, with a flourish, like he was signing the Magna Carta.

"How's everything going?" Shauna asked in a cheerful voice as we moved through the cafeteria line.

"Don't ask," I groaned. I couldn't face the watery cottage cheese special and indulged myself in a large, greasy cheeseburger.

Shauna was sympathetic when I told her about my morning, but she couldn't keep a grin from bubbling to the surface. "But how was your weekend?" she asked. She knew that I had gone out with Ian.

"Terrific. But I'm paying for it today." I paused, wondering if this was the right time to confide in someone. "Shauna," I said. My voice came out in a thin squeak. "Shauna," I repeated, in a stronger tone, "what would you say if . . . if I told you that I may go to school in Paris?"

"What!" She squealed and half the table turned to stare at us.

"Not so loud," I warned her. "I haven't told anyone yet, because it isn't definite, and anyway, I haven't made up my mind. I'm just trying out the idea on you."

"How? When? Why? Tell me!" she demanded in a shrill whisper.

"I may get a scholarship to study dance in Paris. If I go, I'll be sharing a room with Jill Abbott . . . that's the girl in my dance class I told you about, remember? There's a chance that both of us will get scholarships and be gone from November to May."

"Kerry, I don't know what to say." I was surprised to see that her blue eyes were brimming with tears. "I'm really happy for you," she said, dabbing her eyes with her napkin, "but I'll really miss you." She waited a minute, then sniffed noisily. "When will you know?"

"I guess it will be pretty soon. I'm turning in my application form to Miss Beatrice today. It's not definite, but I have an idea that all it takes is a word from her—"

"November to May in Paris!" Shauna blurted out. "I can't believe it."

"Remember, not a word to anyone yet," I cautioned her as the bell rang.

"My lips are sealed," she promised, as we dumped our trays.


Time has a way of standing still when you're waiting for something to happen and whizzing by like a locomotive when you're having a good time. It seemed like an eternity until 2:35 finally came, and then the train ride with Ian went by in a dizzying blur.

We held hands, and Ian gave me a smile that sent a giddy wave of happiness rushing through me. We were almost in Grand Central Station when I remembered to tell him about the audition.

His dark eyes clouded with disappointment, but he quickly recovered his good humor. "I was looking forward to seeing you tonight, Kerry, but I guess I can hold out until tomorrow." He kissed me right on the corner of Forty-Second Street and Fifth Avenue, and my mouth tingled all the way to class.

* * *

I'm never at my best in auditions, and a thin trickle of sweat traveled down my shoulder blades as I waited my turn.

"It's a snap," Jill assured me. "Mr. Rudikoff won't have you do much—a few turns, maybe a *chassé* or two. It's nothing you can't handle, believe me."

We were sitting in the darkened auditorium, waiting for something to happen, when the stage manager came out and introduced himself.

"Hi, I'm Hal," he said. "Everybody should have been given a number when they came in. Just like in a bakery," he added with a grin. "If there's anyone who doesn't have one, see Richie, the assistant manager, right away. He's wearing the red T-shirt, and he's over there in the wings, stage right." He sounded bored, as if he had to give the same spiel every night.

"We'll be auditioning you in groups of four. Please wear ballet shoes when you come on stage." He consulted a clipboard. "Veronica"—he indicated a beautiful woman in a green leotard—"will show you a simple combination, and then we'll ask you to repeat it. Don't be nervous. We're not looking for a finished performance; we just want to get some idea of your technique. And most important of all, we want to see if you can follow directions. So don't give me an *arabesque* if I ask for a *pas de bourrée*, okay?" A nervous titter went through the audience.

He stepped a little closer to the footlights and shielded his eyes from the blinding spotlight trained on him. "Oh, and one other thing. Please don't hound me all night asking how you did. I don't know. Honestly. Mr. Rudikoff makes all the decisions, and the cast list will be posted at nine o'clock. It's final. If you made the show, you'll be on the list. If we need to see you again, or need any other information about you . . . well, like they say, don't call us, we'll call you." This time the ripple of laughter that swept the audience had a slightly desperate edge to it. "I see that the first group is ready to begin, so I'll clear off. Rudy, hit the light." He turned to the piano player. "Max, whenever you're ready."

I was so nervous I didn't hear my number being called, and Jill had to give me a sharp nudge in the ribs. "You're number thirty-three," she said. "Get up there!"

I tried to follow the steps that Veronica showed us, but I felt clumsy and lethargic, as if I were moving underwater in a bad dream. Twice I stumbled doing a *jeté*, and she gave me a funny look, probably wondering why I was wasting my time auditioning. She spent less than ten minutes with us, not nearly enough time to pick up the bewildering array of steps and turns.

"Just remember what you can," she said, stifling a yawn. "When you hear the music, I'm sure it will all come together." She flashed a bright smile, and ushered us on stage, ready to tutor the next group. "Hal," she called, "they're ready. Hit it, Max," she commanded, and the music began.

Luckily my head, neck, arms, and legs seemed to move with a life of their own. Without consciously remembering any of the steps, I somehow tuned into the rhythm of the music, and the combination miraculously followed. I tried to forget the blinding lights, the huge, scary auditorium, and most of all, the invisible eyes that peered critically at us out of the darkness.

The music ended abruptly, and the four of us stood there, uncertain of what to do next. I stared out in the black theater, trying to pick out Jill, but it was impossible. I felt horribly naked and exposed in the harsh lights, conscious of my sweat-stained practice clothes and grimy leg-warmers. After a few minutes, by unspoken agreement, we started to edge offstage.

"Hold it, girls," Hal said. I took a deep breath; my pulse was racing, and my leg muscles were quivering. There was a whispered conference with someone in the audience. "Okay, let's take it from the top, this time with toe shoes. I want to see numbers thirty-four and thirty-three. Thirty-one and thirty-two can leave. Thanks very much, everyone."

Number thirty-four and I scrambled into our toe shoes as the pianist struck up the opening bars again. I didn't know if I could remember the combination a second time, but there was no time to worry about it. When the music ended, there was a long pause, but no whispers from the audience. Finally, I recognized Hal's voice booming out of the darkness. "That's fine, ladies. Next!"

"Was that good or bad?" I asked number thirty-four, a pale blonde with an impossibly frizzed hairdo.

"It was good," she said flatly. "They never ask you to audition twice unless you're good."

"Are you sure?"

She rolled her eyes dramatically to let me know that only an idiot would ask such a question. "If you're lousy, they know it the first time," she said, ending the discussion.

Number thirty-four was right. Both our names appeared on the final cast list, and Jill was so excited, she nearly knocked me over with a bear hug.

"Whoopee!" she said, scanning the rehearsal schedule. "Hey, it looks like this is our last night of freedom, so let's make the most of it. You want to go celebrate? My treat."

"Our last night of freedom? You make it sound like we're condemned prisoners." I laughed, but the sound died in my throat when I looked at the rehearsal times. Every single week night, plus an afternoon and evening rehearsal on Saturdays and Sundays.

"It's worse than I thought," I muttered. Getting the part in *Swan Lake* meant that I had to give up dates with Ian for a while. The flip side of the coin.

"I think I'll pass on the celebrating, Jill. Thanks anyway, but I have a term paper waiting for me at home."

"Oh, sure," she said, looking disappointed. Then she brightened. "We'll have plenty of time to celebrate. After all, we'll be seeing each other at rehearsal every night from now on," she said cheerfully.

"Right," I said, and managed a weak smile. It was easy for Jill to be enthusiastic, I told myself. She didn't have someone like Ian waiting for her.

The next three weeks passed in a blur. I was constantly rehearsing for *Swan Lake*, and Ian didn't take the news well.

"Every night!" he exploded when I told him about the rehearsal schedule. "When will I ever get to see you? I'll have to join the ballet company myself."

I smiled at the idea of Ian, with his carefree, laid-back attitude, ever buckling down to the tough discipline of dancing.

"The rehearsal schedule is terrible, I admit, but it won't go on forever. Don't forget the show is barely a month away."

"A month is a lifetime," he complained. "I want to spend a lot of time with you, Kerry," he said in a softer voice. "I know dancing is important to you, but I thought that I was, too."

"You are. I've . . . I've never met anyone like you," I murmured. I looked at his strong, handsome profile and nearly melted. If only I hadn't auditioned for *Swan Lake* . . . if only I hadn't accepted the part, I caught myself thinking. It was a foolish wish, because dancing was still the most important thing in my life.

"Well," he said slowly, "I guess this means we won't see each other on the train anymore."

"Except on the way into the city," I said, trying to look on the bright side.

"Sure," he said bitterly. "A whole half hour a day. And you'll be so wiped out from your schedule, you'll probably be sleeping or studying." He looked at me thoughtfully. "And weekends are out, aren't they?"

"I'm afraid so," I said, miserable. "I'll just have to

take a lot of rainchecks on Chinatown, and the zoo, and . . ." My voice had a dangerous tremor in it, and I couldn't finish.

We were parked in front of my house, watching a light rain beat a steady rhythm on the windshield.

"You know I care a lot about you, Kerry," he told me.

"It's mutual," I said with a sigh. "In case you hadn't noticed."

"I know I'm being selfish wanting to take up so much of your time, but I can't help it. I never do things halfway, and I want to spend every waking moment with you. Finish *Swan Lake* and come back to me, okay?" He cupped my chin in his hands and looked directly into my eyes.

"I will," I whispered, leaning my head against his chest.

Just then, the Wizard started doing Morse code signals with the porch light, and I knew it was time to go in. "Good-bye, Ian," I said. I gave him a quick kiss and darted up the front steps.

During the days that followed, I missed Ian terribly. He offered to come to the studio, but *Swan Lake* rehearsals were closed to outsiders, and I knew that he would destroy my concentration anyway. Plus it wasn't fair to Ian, I told myself. Why should he have to keep to an insane schedule, just because I chose to?

The rehearsal schedule was cutting into my study time, and before I knew it, I had a new worry: my grades were slipping. Bs were changing into Cs, and then, unbelievably, I got a D on my term paper. I had always done well in English, earning only a few corrections from Miss Tyler's red felt-tipped pen, but the Melville paper was a different story. It had so many bloody red slashes, it looked like Jack the Ripper had gotten to it first. A small, discreet, "See me," was written on the bottom.

Miss Tyler got right to the point when I stayed after class.

"I didn't write out a critique of your paper, Kerry," she began. "Frankly, I didn't know what to say about it."

I could feel myself turning beet-red. I knew that my research had been sloppy, and the writing and typing weren't much better.

She stared at me. "I'd like to ask you a question, though. How much time did you put in on this?"

"Not much," I admitted. "Not because I didn't want to. It's just that with dancing, and traveling to the city . . ."

"You're here to study English, Kerry," she said flatly. "Your academic work has to come first. If I thought that there was an illness, or some extenuating circumstances . . ."

"There isn't," I said, and turned to leave. I could feel tears burning behind my eyes and knew that in another moment they'd spill down my cheeks.

"Kerry." She put her hand gently on my arm. "I want you to see Mrs. Holloway. You've always been a good student, and if your grades are dropping, there must be a reason. Maybe she can help you. You'll like her," she promised.

I saw Mrs. Holloway the next day, and she was much nicer than I had expected. Tall and thin, with laughing brown eyes, she looked more like a college student than a guidance counselor.

"I've been reading your file, Kerry," she said cheerfully. "You've always been a good student."

"Up till now."

She nodded. "I see that there's a problem with Miss Tyler in English. How are your other classes going?"

"Not very well. And once midterms come along . . ." I waved my hand helplessly. "I can barely keep up with my assignments. If I have to start cramming for exams, I don't know what I'll do."

"How is your dancing?" she said, catching me off guard.

"The dancing is great." I was surprised. None of my teachers had ever asked me about it before.

She must have read the question in my eyes because she laughed and said, "There's a notation in your folder that says you catch the afternoon train to Manhattan every day for class."

"Oh." I smiled back at her and relaxed a little.

"You see, Kerry," she said, standing up and reaching for a small coffeepot, "I need to see you as a whole person, not just a high school student, if I'm to be of any help to you. And I've got the feeling that dancing is a very large piece of this person named Kerry Graham. Am I right?"

When I nodded, she handed me a cup of steaming coffee. "Tell me, Kerry, what's the most important thing you'll do today?"

I didn't have to stop and think. "Why, I'll be at dance class this afternoon, and then after that, I'll be rehearsing for *Swan Lake.*"

"You're a serious dancer," she said, her head cocked on one side. The steam from the coffee was rising in gentle swirls around her pixieish face.

"Of course I am," I blurted out. "In fact, I may get a chance to study dance in Paris next month." I hadn't planned on telling her, but she seemed so friendly and interested that the words came out before I could stop them.

I told her about L'Étoile and the scholarship, and she was silent for a few minutes. "Would that solve your problems, do you think?"

"I don't know," I admitted. "I'm sure it would make it easier for me to concentrate on my dancing . . . and I think I could manage my schoolwork easier, too . . . but—"

"But you're not sure you want to leave home?"

"That's right," I said gratefully. "But what else can I do? I can either go to Paris, or quietly flunk out here."

"Kerry," she said, smiling, "someone once said that when you can only think of two options, you aren't thinking hard enough."

"What do you mean?"

"Here's your third option," she said, walking to a sturdy pine bookcase. She handed me a slim yellow book that looked like a college catalog.

"The Professional Children's Institute?" I looked at the address. It was located in midtown Manhattan. "You think this is for me?"

"It could be, Kerry. Take it home and look it over with your parents. I arranged for one of our students to transfer there a couple of years ago."

"A dancer?" I asked, interested.

"No, she was a singer," she said, smiling. "But she was just as dedicated and determined as you are. She graduated with honors, kept up with her music lessons, and the last I heard, she was appearing in an Off-Broadway musical."

The bell rang, summoning me to French class. "Think about it, Kerry, and talk to your parents. I'll be here whenever you need me."

# Chapter 10

"What do you think?" I asked anxiously. Mom and Dad were sitting in the den looking over the catalog from the Professional Children's Institute.

"It's a possibility. Definitely," my father said, adjusting his glasses. "I like the idea that the students are given a lot of leeway to pursue their professional careers."

"Yet they still can earn a high school diploma," my mother added.

My parents had met with Miss Holloway earlier in the day, and she had explained that the institute was geared to students who were also performers. Schedules were flexible, with classes repeated several times a day, so students could be free to attend rehearsals and auditions.

"The main thing, Kerry, is how do *you* feel about it?"

As usual, Dad went to the heart of the matter. The truth was, I didn't know how I felt. Part of me wanted to jump at the chance to enroll at PCI as soon as I could. For five days a week, my life would be devoted primarily to dance. I'd travel to the city every day and divide my time between Miss Beatrice's and PCI. Most of the instructors at PCI were involved in the performing arts, so they tended to be more easygoing than teachers in a traditional high school. I'd have more time during the day to take dance classes, and perhaps even explore other studios and styles of teaching.

On the weekends, I'd have time for Ian.

We could go out for pizza, catch up on horror movies, and maybe even play chess with the Wizard on rainy Saturdays. It sounded blissful, the best of both worlds, and yet . . .

Paris! What was it Jill had called it? The most romantic city in the world. A place for poets and dreamers. If I turned down the chance to go, would I ever get another one? Maybe life would interfere, like it had with my mother, and I'd have to forego my dreams.

It would be fun to explore the city with Jill on our time off. I could already picture us strolling up and down the Champs-Élysées, peeking into expensive boutiques, buying croissants from a sidewalk vendor. Art galleries . . . museums . . . midnight in a tiny cafe. And to think that I might actually win a scholarship to L'Étoile! Some of the top instructors in the world taught there. How could I say no to an opportunity like that?

"I need to think it over," I said slowly to my parents. "And I need to talk to some more people."

"You also need to be offered the scholarship," the Wizard reminded me. We all laughed. He had a way of getting to the heart of the matter, too.

I decided to retrace my steps and go back to the people whose advice I had sought earlier.

I had a long talk with Miss Beatrice, and came closer to understanding her than I ever had. She tried to be impartial, but I could tell that she felt I belonged in Paris with Jill.

"What has it been like for you? Being a dancer, I mean." She didn't answer me for a minute, and I studied her. It was strange. I had known Miss Beatrice for four years, and yet I didn't really know her at all. It was hard to imagine her ever having dreams or disappointments, or even having a life outside the studio. I knew that she was single and lived in a small apartment in Soho.

"It's been . . . hard," she said. We were sitting in her tiny office. Class was over, and Jill had dashed out to a coffee shop to buy us sandwiches before we started rehearsal. "Does that surprise you?" She smiled and patted her face with a towel. Under the harsh fluorescent light, she looked drawn and tired. It was impossible to guess her age, but someone said that she had been dancing for twenty years. A long career for a dancer.

"It gets harder every year," she said, as if she were reading my thoughts.

"You're not sorry you chose to be a dancer, are you?"

"No, I wouldn't have wanted it any other way. I've been lucky, Kerry, because I've done what I wanted to do. I had a goal, and I think I've fulfilled it."

"Dancing is really your life, isn't it?" I said, understanding it for the first time.

"Oh, yes. It has to be," she said quietly. "You see, if you're going to be a dancer, you can't possibly want to be anything else. Dancing has to be the most important thing in the world to you. Every-

thing else must come second. A home . . . family
. . . friends."

Friends. I thought of Ian, and a dizzying wave of
longing swept through me. "You're my favorite person," he had said to me on the train earlier that
night. "My favorite person in the whole world," he
had repeated, giving me a lingering kiss. How
could I ever put Ian in second place? I wondered.
Didn't he deserve to be first—always?

I forced him out of my mind. "You've been successful," I said to Miss Beatrice, stating a fact.

She laughed wearily. "Successful? Yes. And I've
failed a lot, too."

"Not you!" I blurted out.

"Of course," she said calmly. "I haven't danced
some of the parts that I've wanted to, and now I'm
too old." I knew what she meant. Dancers have
long years of practice, and then only a brief, golden
time when they are at their peak. "There have been
disappointments," she went on. "And pain. But I
suppose you know about that already," she said
wryly.

I nodded. I had twisted my ankle doing a *jeté*
during rehearsal, and it had throbbed steadily ever
since.

"The body gets older; it rebels. I go to the barre
every morning, and some days, it's pure torture.
You've been a dancer long enough to know that you
have to be prepared to always be in pain somewhere. You've just got to accept it," she sighed.

"I'm glad I had you as my teacher," I said suddenly. "Whatever happens from here on in."

A smile lit up her face, and suddenly she didn't
seem so tired. "I'm glad. It's students like you and

Jill who make it all worthwhile, you know. The gifted ones."

"I hope you're right."

"I am," she said. "You have the determination to make it, and the talent. It takes both, of course. Without the gift, it's just technique, just acrobatics. But if you dance and hear the inner music in your soul . . ." She stared out at the grimy city street below, lost in her own thoughts.

She never finished the sentence because Jill arrived breathlessly with our dinner. Two cheeseburgers. Stone cold.

"I had a nice chat with your parents," Miss Holloway told me the next day. "They're very proud of you, you know."

I nodded. "And they're leaving the decision up to me."

"They trust you, Kerry." She paused. "Are you any closer to making up your mind? It wouldn't hurt to start lining up your courses, if you've definitely decided on PCI."

"No, let's hold off on that for a while. I still haven't heard anything on the scholarship."

"Are you leaning that way? I mean, if it comes through?" she asked, smiling.

I shrugged helplessly. "I wish I knew which way I'm leaning. I'm going to have to pick petals off a daisy to decide, I guess." I was only half kidding. How could I ever make up my mind when both choices seemed right?

"Well, you'll probably have a few more days to mull it over," she told me. "You'll probably get a call about the scholarship when you least expect it. And that's when you'll have to move."

She was right. The next night I saw Miss Beatrice sitting in the audience when I was rehearsing *Swan Lake*. I was so surprised that I bumped into Jill in the middle of a *pas de bourrée* and earned a reprimand from Mr. Rudikoff.

"Sorry," I muttered, trying not to stare at Miss Beatrice. What a way to show off for my teacher!

As soon as we had a break, Miss Beatrice rushed up to us. "It's here," she said in a low voice.

"The scholarship?" I tried to speak normally, but I sounded as if I was talking from the bottom of the ocean.

"Yes." Then her face broke in a wide beam. She turned to Jill and embraced both of us in a huge hug. "You both made it. I knew you would." There were more hugs and exclamations, and Jill started crying.

Our moment of triumph was short-lived, though, because Mr. Rudikoff called us right back to rehearsal. With the performance only two nights away, he was determined to make every second count.

The fact that I had really won the scholarship didn't hit me until I was on the train home, later that night. I stared out the window, watching the lights of the city race by, and felt more confused and alone than I ever had in my life.

Paris. Ian. PCI. New York. Miss Beatrice. My thoughts were so jumbled, I knew I'd never straighten them out. At least not that night. I was so afraid to make a commitment, so afraid to make the wrong decision.

Without even meaning to, I pulled a coin from my pocket. What was it Ian had said? *Flip a coin. Let heads be choice "A", tails be choice "B". If you're happy with the decision, then it's what you really wanted all along. If you're unhappy . . .*

"Heads I go to Europe, tails I stay in New York and go to PCI." The coin glinted in the air, then fell into my palm. Heads. Paris. Was I happy? I frowned and tried to think.

"Take a few days and think about it," my mother said at breakfast the following morning. I was exhausted, mentally and physically.

"In fact, I wouldn't even try to make any decision until *Swan Lake* is over," she added. "At least you know you've got the scholarship if you want it, and Miss Holloway can easily set up a transfer to PCI. So it's really your choice, Kerry. You're holding all the cards."

"Maybe you're right," I said wearily. I was so tired, I could hardly concentrate on what she was saying. One thing I knew for sure, though: I couldn't keep up this schedule much longer. I had lost ten pounds in a month, and my eyes were ringed with dark circles all the time.

"Just give it a rest, honey," she said, staring at me. "You've been pushing yourself so hard lately. Put your mind on hold for a couple of days, okay? The decision will keep."

"Hey, you look wiped out," Ian said to me on the

train that day. "You could play Giselle's ghost without makeup."

"Thanks."

"I'm only kidding," he said, pulling me next to him on the seat. "But I'm worried about you. You know what you need when the show is over? A lot of time with me. Here's my prescription: long restful afternoons at the movies . . . relaxing little lunches in Greenwich Village . . . or, hey, I know. How about a boat ride up to Bear Mountain? They say a sea voyage will cure anything."

"The Hudson River isn't the ocean."

"We'll use our imaginations," he said.

"Ian, what night are you coming to see the show?" *Swan Lake* was running for five nights straight.

"Every night," he said, smiling.

"Such devotion!" I teased him.

"You're absolutely right. It's the only way I'll get to see you."

"The first night might be the best. Everyone's energy is always up."

He shook his head. "No, the last night will be the best," he said solemnly. "Because that's when I'll get my girl back." He shot me a meaningful look, and I didn't dare reply.

Two days later, I came to a decision. It was early morning, and I felt strangely refreshed and bursting with energy, even though I had gotten only a few hours of sleep the night before. They say that your unconscious mind works on your problems while you sleep, and it must be true, because everything was suddenly clear to me.

"You look better today, honey," my mother said. "I'll be thinking about you tonight," she added, smiling. I've always been superstitious about opening nights, so I had asked Mom, Dad, and Daniel to come to the show on the second night.

Tonight I wanted to see Ian alone.

*Swan Lake* unfolded like a beautiful dream.

I saw Jill backstage before the show started. We were crowded in the wings with the rest of the dancers, poised like horses at the starting gate.

"I can't believe it," she said, her face aglow with excitement. I didn't know whether she meant appearing in *Swan Lake* or winning the Paris scholarship.

I was about to ask her, but just then Mr Rudikoff appeared next to us, counting softly under his breath. "Five, six, seven, eight, and—"

The conductor raised his baton, a hush fell over the audience, and the curtains opened. It was time for the first group of dancers to move on stage.

Everyone has their own interpretation of *Swan Lake*, but I think Mr. Rudikoff's was as close to perfection as you can get. Natalie Petrov's performance was fantastic. Dancers usually become expert in either *allegro*, which is fast, or *adagio*, a slow, lyrical type of dance. Natalie tended toward *adagio*, and it was smooth and flowing. She moved so effortlessly, she reminded me of an enchanted, birdlike creature floating in space.

I caught a glimpse of Jill gliding across the floor. She had a little secret smile on her face, as if she were listening to the "inner music" that Miss Beatrice talked about.

I didn't have time to concentrate on her, though, because before I knew it, it was my turn. I drew a breath, yielded to the pulsing rhythm from the orchestra pit, and began to dance.

Judging from the number of curtain calls, the ballet was a tremendous success. All of us lined up on stage, doing the wilt-and-blossom routine that Mr. Rudikoff had taught us. When the curtain fell, we resembled wilting flowers, heads drooping, arms hanging limply at our sides. When the curtain swung open, we miraculously sprang to life, heads up, smiles firmly in place.

The curtain calls went on and on; the applause was thundering. I was thrilled at the warm reception we were getting, but I was also eager to get off the stage. Finally the applause died down, and I scurried back to the dressing room. I smeared a thick dollop of cold cream on my face to remove the stage makeup, then headed for the shower.

Moments later, I pulled a soft knit dress over my head and hurried to the lobby to find Ian. The lobby was jammed with well-wishers, and I had to fight my way through the crowd.

A familiar arm slid around my waist. "You were fantastic," he said, giving me a big hug. "The best one up there."

"On stage, we all look alike," I told him. It was true. Mr. Rudikoff insisted that we wear our hair in tight chignons and use identical makeup. From a distance we could have been clones.

"I'd know you anywhere," he protested. "You were the third tutu from the left."

"I was the fourth."

"That's what I meant to say," he added breezily. We had to practically shout over the buzz of conversation, and he pulled me aside. "Is it true that dancers are always starving after they give a performance? Because I know a terrific little Indian restaurant not far from here . . ."

"It's true," I assured him. "And I'm in a mood to celebrate."

The restaurant was small, cozy, and dimly lit. Ian and I sat close together in a corner booth, and he ordered chicken curry for both of us. As soon as the waitress left, he leaned across the table and kissed me. It was awfully hard to break away. But I knew that I had to speak up right away.

"Ian," I said. I reached over and took his strong hand in mine. "There's something I have to tell you."

*What do you think Kerry should do?*

*If you think she should go to the Professional Children's Institute and stay closer to home and to Ian, turn the page to Ending 1.*

*If you think she should accept the scholarship to study in Paris, even if it means leaving Ian, turn to Ending 2 on page 139.*

# Ending 1

"It sounds serious. What is it, Kerry?" His hand closed over mine, and the corners of his mouth curved in a heart-tugging smile. I looked into those melting gray eyes, and I knew I had made the right decision.

"I won't be seeing you on the two thirty-five anymore, Ian."

"No?"

"No. I've decided to change schools. Starting next week, I'll be at the Professional Children's Institute in Manhattan."

His face lit up, and he let out a whistle. "I was afraid you were going to say something earth-shattering—that you were moving to California or Alaska. But the Professional Children's Institute! That's terrific news, Kerry. You know, some of the kids who work on the soaps went there." He leaned over and gave me a quick kiss. "You don't know how relieved I am," he said with a sheepish smile. "I thought for a minute you were going to say you didn't want to see me anymore."

"Not see you anymore!"

"Never mind. I'm paranoid." He gave my hand a squeeze. "When did all this happen?"

"I made up my mind a couple of days ago. There was another possibility, but this seemed like the right thing to do."

"It is," he said warmly. "You're really going to love it there. You'll be around a lot of talented kids, and you'll pick up a lot of tips. If you're serious about being a performer, that's the place to be. At least, that's what Janice always said."

"Janice?" An image of someone tall and slender with cascading hair crossed my mind. I tried to ignore the little pinprick of jealousy that stabbed my heart.

"My cousin," he said patiently. "She spent a year at PCI."

He gave an angelic smile that was absolutely irresistible.

"Oh." I smiled back at him, feeling more friendly to Cousin Janice.

"So your schedule will be completely different. They have class from eight to twelve, don't they?"

"Right. I'll have a three-hour break between PCI and Miss Beatrice's to study or go to auditions, or even to take another dance class."

"This is fantastic, Kerry. Things will be so much better for us, you know? We'll have a lot more time together. Maybe you won't have to rush back home every day, and I can show you around New York."

"I'd like that," I told him. His eyes were bright with excitement.

"The weekends will be great, too—you won't be working all the time. There are dozens of places I want to take you. I bet you've never had dinner at the Automat, for example. They've got the best macaroni and cheese in town."

"Never."

He shook his head sadly. "And you've probably never gotten over to the Metropolitan to see the Egyptian collection—the Temple of Dendur is fabulous. And the medieval armor—I don't suppose you've ever seen that?"

"Afraid not," I said, smiling.

"Your education has been sadly neglected, then. I hate to ask, but have you ever gone for a ride on the Staten Island ferry?"

"Nope."

"Ridden the carousel in Central Park? Gone to the Bronx Zoo?"

I shook my head.

"It's going to be hard to know where to start," he sighed happily. "It will take years to show you all the sights," he promised.

"We've got plenty of time," I said, as he slid his arm around me.

Our dinner arrived just then, and we both grinned when we saw how delicious it looked. Of course, I'd never had Indian food before in my life. Yet again, Ian was introducing me to wonderful new things.

"How did it go?" Mom and Dad asked in unison the moment I unlocked the front door.

"She was brilliant," Ian assured them. "Six curtain calls."

"A few of those were for Natalie Petrov," I told them with a grin.

Mom hung up our coats and smiled at us. "I'll bet you two are starving."

I looked at Ian and we burst out laughing, remembering all the food we had had for dinner. "We ate, but maybe if there's any of that chocolate cake left . . ."

"I'll get it, Kerry. You just sit down and relax; you must be exhausted."

"I've got to take my shoes off," I said apologetically to Ian, as I curled up on the sofa. My feet were throbbing from the viselike grip of the satin toe shoes, and I rubbed them gently. I tried not to look at the bumps and swellings—at the rate I was going, I'd need a personal chiropodist before long.

"You're still keyed up after being on stage, aren't you, Kerry?" Dad asked.

I nodded. Miss Beatrice says that performing is like having an atomic reactor inside you. It sets up a chain reaction that takes hours to cool down. Even though I was motionless, I could still feel the adrenaline surging through me, still feel the music pulsing through my veins.

Dad and Ian chatted for a few minutes, and then Dad excused himself to call a client. I was just going to move a little closer to Ian on the sofa when the Wizard spoke up.

"Are you any good at Defender?"

"I almost cleared a million the last time I played," Ian said, shrugging his shoulders. The Wizard was obviously impressed. "That was quite a game," Ian went on. "I was on the eightieth attack wave—"

"Wow! Want to play now?" The Wizard was already scrambling to his feet.

"Sure." Ian flashed me a quick smile. "You don't mind, do you, Kerry?"

"Of course not," I said. I smothered a sigh and stood up. "I'll help Mom in the kitchen."

She was cutting thick slabs of chocolate cake and topping them with ice cream.

"Well, you've made up your mind, haven't you?"

"It shows?"

"You don't have that worried, haunted look anymore." She paused. "Unless you're just relieved that opening night is over."

"No, it wasn't opening night that was bothering me. I was going crazy trying to decide between Paris and PCI. But I know what I want to do, Mom. I want to go to PCI."

"Oh, Kerry, that's wonderful news. I'm happy for you," she said, hugging me. "It's surprising how many people know about the school, and all the famous alumni they have. I was talking to Adele Trenton today, and she said that her daughter went there a few years ago. She said it changed her whole life. She's a cellist now with the Boston Pops." She filled the coffeepot and turned to me. "When do you think you can start there?"

"I'd like to start right away. Next week is the end of a grading period at school, so it would make things simpler. I'll talk to Mrs. Holloway on Monday and see what she says."

We heard an ecstatic shout from Ian followed by a chortle from the Wizard. "There goes another humanoid!"

"I wish I could lure Ian away from that game," I muttered.

My mother picked up the dessert tray and

headed for the den. "Kerry, I hate to tell you this," she whispered, "but there are some things in life you just can't compete with." She winked at me like a conspirator, and I started to smile.

"You really were great tonight," Ian told me when we were finally alone. He touched a match to some kindling, and soon the firelight gave the room an amber glow. Mom, Dad, and the Wizard had gone to bed, and Ian and I were sitting close together on the sofa.

"I think you're a little prejudiced," I said lightly. "After all, I'm just a chorus dancer. Practically anonymous."

"Not to me, you're not. When you're on stage, I don't notice anyone else." He bent close to me and nuzzled my neck. His skin was smooth and warm, and smelled faintly of lemon after-shave. "I'm still curious about something, though. You told me in the restaurant that there was another possibility. What did you mean?"

"I was thinking of going to Paris," I said softly. The idea seemed farfetched, incredible, here in this cozy room with the flickering firelight.

For once Ian was speechless. He dropped his arm from my shoulder, and looked at me in amazement.

"I was offered a scholarship," I explained.

"I know this sounds selfish, but I'm glad you didn't take it," he said.

"I am too." I was telling the truth. "At first, it seemed too good to resist, but the more I thought about it, the more I realized what I would have to give up. I've got a terrific family . . . and friends."

He let his lips graze my cheek. "I hope I'm your number one friend," he said softly.

"Of course."

"For all time?"

"For all time."

He bent down and kissed me, and I knew I had done the right thing.


"When's the big day?" Shauna asked me. She mouthed the words silently like a ventriloquist, under the watchful eye of Miss Simmons, the homeroom teacher.

"Next Monday," I mouthed back.

"So Friday will be your last day here?" she hissed. She gave a theatrical grimace. "I'm really going to miss you. But I've got some good news," she said, brightening. "I want to have a party for you."

"A party?" It was an effort to talk out of the side of my mouth, and I was wishing the dismissal bell would ring.

"A farewell party. I'll ask Maria and Trixie, and anyone else you want to have. We can have it this Saturday. I've already checked with my parents."

I smiled at her. "This is really nice of you, Shauna."

"Not so nice," she said with a grin. "I'm dying to get a look at Ian. In fact, everyone is. Just think, the boy you gave up Paris for," she said dreamily. "I'll bet he's really something."

A shadow fell across my notebook. Miss Simmons had swooped down on us like a falcon. "Do you girls know what the penalty is for talking during homeroom?"

Teachers love questions like that. Shauna and I waited to see what would happen next. We both knew that the penalty was a fifteen-minute detention period after school.

"But this is an emergency," Shauna said plaintively.

"An emergency." Miss Simmons raised her carefully tweezed eyebrow. She had an "I've-heard-it-all" look on her face.

"This is Kerry's last week here. She's transferring to the Professional Children's Institute in Manhattan next Monday. We were just planning a farewell party for her."

"Oh." Miss Simmons' expression softened. "I've heard of PCI," she said. "I didn't know you were leaving us, Kerry. I certainly wish you luck in your new school. That's a school for performing students, isn't it? What exactly do you . . . uh, do?"

"I'm a dancer?"

"A dancer," she repeated slowly. Clearly, she didn't know what to say next. Finally, she said, "Well, good luck to you, Kerry. I think we can forget about the detention in view of the circumstances."

She permitted herself a thin, frosty smile. "I'll watch for your name on Broadway," she said.

The bell rang just then, and she charged back up the aisle to her post.

"You should have told her you were a *ballet* dancer, Kerry," Shauna whispered as we gathered our books.

"Why?" I whispered back.

"Because she probably thinks you're the kind who wears tassels and pops out of cakes!"

We held on to each other, giggling, and staggered out into the hall.

"You've made up your mind," Miss Holloway said delightedly.

I laughed. "It must be pretty obvious. My mother said the same thing to me."

She motioned me to a bean-bag chair and perched on the edge of her desk. "You look like someone has just lifted a hundred-pound weight from those skinny shoulders of yours," she teased me.

"I'll bet you know what I've decided."

"You're going to PCI."

"You're psychic," I told her.

"No, I'm not psychic. Just observant. Plus I just took a course in nonverbal communication. Body language."

"Body language? What do you mean?"

"You learn to read people's gestures and expressions just as if you were reading a book. And performers—like you, Kerry—are the most expressive people of all. Your gestures were a lot more revealing than your words."

"What did I do?"

She paced the room with a thoughtful look on her face. "Whenever you mentioned PCI, you had a big grin on your face, and when you talked about Paris, you got a kind of lost, worried expression. In fact, I started to wonder if maybe you hoped you wouldn't even be offered the scholarship. That way, you wouldn't have to decide whether or not to accept it."

"I think you're right. But I was offered it, you know."

"And you turned it down." She nodded as if she understood.

"It's hard to explain," I said. "I realized that there are so many wonderful things going on for me right here. I love studying with Miss Beatrice, and New York is one of the dance capitals of the world. And there are my parents and friends . . ."

"You'll have the best of both worlds," she said encouragingly.

"I think so. At least I hope I will."

"Incidentally, you won't have to audition to get in. When I told them you were in *Swan Lake*, they were really impressed."

"So there won't be any problem in my starting there next term?"

"You're on your way, Kerry."

"Did you tell your parents about Paris?" Jill asked me.

I drew a halting breath, dreading what must come next. "Yes, but I've decided not to go. I'm going to transfer to the Professional Children's Institute instead. It's a school for performers—"

"Yes, yes, I've heard of it," she said impatiently. "How can you turn down Paris? Are you sure you've really given it enough thought?"

"I've thought about it," I said quietly. "And it's just not the thing for me now."

Jill rested her leg casually on a waist-high folding table and began massaging a muscle in her thigh. "But, Kerry," she protested, "dancing is your whole life. What made you change your mind?"

How could I make her understand? "Jill, dancing *has* been my whole life. It will always be a large part of it, but . . . people change. I've changed a lot in the past few weeks—I've seen a whole new side of myself."

"It's Ian, isn't it?" Her pale eyes rested on me accusingly.

"Partly," I admitted. "But that's not the whole story. I guess the truth is that I've found out there are some things I'm not willing to miss out on, even for dancing."

"Nothing can be as important as dancing," she said flatly. She tossed her long blond ponytail and walked away.

I made two friends on my first day at PCI: Laura Ashton, a bubbly redhead who was studying acting, and Jennifer Warren, a slim brunette who wanted to be a jazz dancer.

"If you've been studying with Miss Beatrice, you're in good shape," Laura told me. "Everyone in town knows she's the best."

Laura and Jennifer were giving me the grand tour of the school, and we decided to start with lunch in the downstairs cafeteria.

"The only thing I can't understand," Jennifer piped up, "is why you haven't been making the rounds before this."

"Making the rounds?"

"Going to auditions. Casting calls. Visiting agents."

"I never had the chance. The minute dancing

class was over, I had to rush back to Bronxville and get started on my homework."

"Well, it's going to be different here at PCI," Laura promised me. "Performing comes first. Jennifer and I will be glad to show you the ropes. In fact, we can get started today, unless you've got other plans. I was going to do a voice-over, but it was cancelled."

"Hey, that reminds me," Jennifer said. "Has anyone checked the casting notices in *Backstage* today?"

"There's nothing there. I looked in *Show Business* too. We're too young for that new show they're casting at the Winter Garden." I must have looked blank because she turned to me and smiled. "You have to check the trade papers every week, Kerry," she explained. "And keep your ears open when you go to auditions. That's the only way you find out what's going on in town."

I nodded, feeling a little overwhelmed. Voice-overs, agents, making the rounds, casting notices. I clearly had a lot to learn.

We had just finished a particularly grueling dance routine, and were preparing to start another, when Miss Beatrice signaled to the piano player. We stopped dancing and stared at her in surprise.

"We're breaking up a little early today, girls," she said in a breathless voice. She had been demonstrating pirouettes and her face was flushed and shiny. "Everybody gather around," she called to the girls at the far end of the rehearsal room. "I have an announcement to make."

Without meaning to, I glanced at Jill and saw that she was as surprised as I was. Jill and I had avoided each other since the day I told her I wouldn't be going to Paris—whenever our eyes met, she gave me a chilly look and turned away.

There was a buzz of excited conversation, and Miss Beatrice held up her hand for silence. "Girls," she said softly, "this is a happy occasion." She was looking at Jill.

Suddenly I understood. "Today I want to toast a very special student, Jill Abbott. As you all know, Jill has won a scholarship to L'Étoile, which is one of the most famous dance schools in Paris. I'm very proud of her, and I know you are, too."

She beamed at Jill, and everyone started applauding. "I know you want to wish her well before she leaves us," Miss Beatrice said loudly, "so I've arranged for some refreshments for a little party. I need some help with the food. Kerry . . ." she said, since I was standing close to her.

"Of course," I said quickly. We walked the length of the room to her office, and I glanced over my shoulder at the mob surrounding Jill. She was swamped with hugs and congratulations. "I'd give my life to go to Paris," I heard someone say. "Where will you be living?" "You'll meet a Frenchman on a Moped and you'll never make it to class," someone teased her.

Maybe the expression on my face gave me away, because Miss Beatrice touched my arm. "You're not having any regrets, are you? Any second thoughts?"

I hesitated. "I'd like to say no, none at all." We

127

started taking the covers off platters of tiny sandwiches.

"But you can't," she said wisely.

"No," I admitted. "I guess I'll never be a hundred percent sure I'm doing the right thing. I've gone over and over it, and I keep getting the same answer: I should stay in New York and go to PCI."

"But still . . ."

"But still there's a little nagging voice that tells me that Paris is the most exciting city in the world, and only an idiot would turn it down." I reached for a bag of napkins and looked at her. "Do you think everyone has those little nagging voices that tell them they should have done something different? Do you ever feel that way?"

"Of course, Kerry." Her voice was surprisingly gentle. "When I was young, my favorite poem was 'The Road Not Taken' by Robert Frost. Do you know it? 'Two roads diverged in a wood, and I—I took the one less traveled by, and that has made all the difference.' You see, it's about a man standing at a crossroads. No matter which way he turns, he'll always wonder where the other road would have taken him. Would he be happier or wiser if he had taken the other way? Who knows?" She shrugged. "It wasn't until I got older that I really appreciated what Frost was talking about."

I was hoping she'd say more, but just then a girl stuck her head in the door. "Need any help? The natives are getting restless."

"No, we're all ready, if you'll pick up one of those platters. Let's get on with the party!"

It was a typical dancer's party. Low-fat cream cheese on tiny rounds of diet wheat bread, paper-thin slices of cheddar cheese on melba toast, fresh fruit and diet drinks. Miss Beatrice never believed that a social occasion was an excuse to break training.

We sat on the floor, and the conversation was peppered with questions for Jill. She fielded them shyly. Yes, the scholarship included her tuition and room and board. No, she would not be living on campus. She would live at a pension, a type of boardinghouse for students. No, her French wasn't the greatest, but she hoped to take a quick course at Berlitz as soon as she got there.

"This is your last night with us, right?" someone said.

Jill nodded, and I thought that her eyes looked suspiciously moist. Most of us had been together at Miss Beatrice's for three or four years: we shared the same dreams. We were a close-knit group.

"We'll miss you, Jill," Cindy said quietly, and there was a chorus of agreement.

"I'll miss all of you," Jill answered, and she blinked rapidly a few times. "I'll miss all the hours we spent here practicing . . . and Miss Beatrice . . . and everybody," she said, looking directly at me.

Later, when we were picking up the glasses and plates, Jill came over to me. "I hope we're still friends, Kerry," she said in a little voice. "I didn't want to leave without saying good-bye and wishing you luck at PCI." She looked worried, as if she were afraid I'd walk away.

I smiled at her. "I'm glad to hear you say that. I didn't want you to leave without things being settled between us. After all, Paris shouldn't break up a friendship, should it?"

129

"No, it shouldn't." She hugged me, then stepped back and looked at me, her gray eyes pale and serious. "I was so disappointed when I realized that you weren't going to come with me. But you know something, Kerry? It finally dawned on me that what's right for me isn't necessarily right for you."

"And Paris is right for you, isn't it? I mean, you're sure about it?"

"Oh, yes," she said, and there was no hesitation in her voice. "I'm a hundred percent sure. I can hardly wait to get on that plane."

"I'll expect a full report on L'Étoile," I told her.

"Oh, you'll get it. I'll give you the inside story on Paris, and you can keep me posted about PCI and New York. A deal?"

"You've got it," I said, and we hugged each other again.

Jill's words rang in my ears as I took the train home to Bronxville that night. I'm a hundred percent sure, she had said.

It must be nice to be that sure of something.


I may have had some lingering doubts whether I'd done the right thing, but I knew for sure that life got a lot easier after I started at PCI. I had more free time than ever before, and yet I seemed to be accomplishing everything I wanted to. It was as if someone had waved a magic wand. Suddenly, all the little pieces of my life fell into place.

Ian loved the new arrangement. "You seem a lot happier," he said to me one crisp day in China-town. We were sitting in a cheerful little restaurant on Mott Street, surrounded by enough food to feed an army. "You sure are a lot more relaxed than you used to be."

I laughed, remembering how I used to divide my day into one-hour intervals. "I was pretty compulsive, wasn't I?"

"But lovable," he said, making a fresh attack on his fried rice.

Ian had insisted that I sample Cantonese cooking and had ordered diced chicken with peanuts, bean curd with shredded pork, and something called thousand year egg. "It's not what it sounds like," he told me with a wink.

"Thank goodness!" I said. My stomach had turned over a little when I heard the name.

"Admit it, it's pretty good, isn't it?" He waved his fork toward the little dishes of chopped vegetables and chicken.

"It's great. You're a lot more adventurous than I am. I never would have ordered anything like this. Don't forget I've been eating broiled flounder with lemon most of my life."

"Just think, Kerry, without me, you never would have learned to eat with chopsticks."

"And without me, you never would have learned to like ballet."

"True," he admitted. "Let's face it, we're a perfect combination. I sure am glad you didn't go to Paris." Then he hesitated. "Are you glad, too?"

"Of course I am," I assured him quickly.

"Then swear that you'd rather be sitting here in a Chinese restaurant with me than in a café on the Champs-Élysées," he teased me.

"I swear," I said, holding up one hand like a boy scout. "I'd rather be sitting here with you," I repeated. It wasn't exactly a lie, but it wasn't the whole truth, either. Visions of red-checkered table-clothes and broad avenues and boat rides on the Seine still drifted through my mind. I shook my head and willed them to go away. There would be other chances to go to Paris, wouldn't there? Ian smiled at me and I felt a sudden rush of love for him.

"Where to?" he asked when we stepped outside. It was early afternoon, and the bright sunlight brought the twisted streets of Chinatown into sharp focus.

"Why don't we walk to Washington Square, then take a bus up Sixth Avenue and do some window-shopping?" I suggested.

The bus filled quickly with shoppers, and Ian and I were squeezed together on the front seat. Neither of us minded a bit, and Ian slid his arm around me as we peered out the window at the fabulous window displays.

"New York has got to be the most exciting city in the world," Ian commented.

I smiled and didn't say anything. I was trying hard not to imagine what it would be like shopping in Paris, dashing into little bakeries for hot loaves of crusty French bread . . . or maybe sampling perfumes at some tiny shop. . . .

"Seen enough?" Ian asked, interrupting my thoughts. We were near Central Park.

Suddenly I had an idea. "Let's go to the Metropolitan, okay? I want to see that Egyptian exhibit you told me about."

"Hey, that's a great idea! You'll love it."

I had a special reason for wanting to go to the

Metropolitan Museum that day—I wanted to buy Ian a present. The last time we had been there, Ian had admired a Toulouse-Lautrec poster, and I was determined to get it for him.

As soon as we got to the Egyptian Room, I told Ian I had to make a phone call, and I dashed down to the museum gift shop. I rifled through racks of posters, but after a discouraging ten minutes I gave up. The poster wasn't there.

"The Lautrec poster?" the woman behind the counter said thoughtfully. "No, we're sold out of that one, I'm sure of it. But there are some marvelous Van Goghs and Gauguins if you'd like to see them."

I shook my head, ready to leave, when something in the display case caught my eye. It was a tiny pottery horse, painted in brilliant colors. I knew that I had to buy it for Ian.

"The horse," I said, pointing. "What is it?"

The woman unlocked the case and lifted it out. "Isn't it lovely? It's a reproduction of an ancient Chinese sculpture. Would you like to hold it?"

I ran my hand over it admiringly. It was the perfect gift for Ian because it would remind him of the day we met. "Remember the name of Caligula's horse," he had told me on the train.

"I'll take it," I said. I could hardly wait to show it to Ian.

"That was a long phone call," he said suspiciously when I rejoined him.

"I had a lot to say." I smiled and took his hand. "Why don't we stop for some hot chocolate and look at the Egyptian Room later."

"You're certainly acting mysterious today," he

told me when we sat down. "In fact," he said with a grin, "you're acting so funny that maybe this isn't the best time to give you your present."

"My present?"

"You've heard of going-away presents? This is a 'I'm-glad-you-decided-to-stay-home' present."

He handed me a little velvet box. "Open it," he said softly.

I lifted out a gold medallion suspended from a delicate chain. It was inscribed in French. "More than yesterday . . ." I said, translating it.

"More than yesterday, less than tomorrow. That's how much I love you, in case you didn't know it. And I had it written in French because . . . well, who knows, maybe we'll go to Paris together someday." He rested his hand on mine, and I felt a lump start to rise in my throat. "I know how tempted you were to go to Paris this time, Kerry, but I swear you won't regret staying here."

"It's beautiful, Ian. I love it," I managed to say.

"Let me put it on for you." He fastened it, and let his hand linger on my neck for a moment.

"I almost forgot. I got a present for you, too. That was the long phone call," I told him sheepishly.

I gave him the horse, and his face broke into a smile. "Hey, this is great!" he said, examining it carefully. But I could tell he didn't know what it meant.

"Doesn't it remind you of anything?" I said pointedly. He obviously didn't have a clue what I was getting at.

"The day we met?" I said impatiently. "Caligula's horse, remember? You told me that I should always remember the name of Caligula's horse."

"Oh, yeah!" He put the horse on the table and moved a little closer to me. His lips were just inches from mine.

"So did you ever learn the name of his horse?" His voice was low, and I felt a little shiver go through me.

"Uh, no . . ." I said in an unsteady voice. He was staring at me with those gorgeous eyes, and I could hardly catch my breath.

"Shame on you. It's really something you should know," he said. "It might come in handy some-time." He leaned closer.

"I'm sure you're right."

I never had the chance to ask him what it was, though, because just then he kissed me, and all thoughts of Roman emperors and famous horses flew out of my head.

The pale blue air mail envelope was covered with exotic stamps.

"Can I have the stamps?" the Wizard asked, examining the envelope.

"It's from Jill," I said, snatching it away from him. "And if you let me read it in peace, you'll get the stamps."

Jill's writing was bold, flamboyant. "Paris is fab-ulous!" she wrote. "The classes at L'Étoile are tops, and I even got a compliment on my *arabesques*. Not to mention all the extracurricular activities, including a midnight boat ride on the Seine with a new friend I met at the pension. It was like some-thing out of a movie! Paris is everything I thought it would be, and more. You'd love it here, Kerry. You really would!"

I know I would I agreed silently. Paris sounded wonderful, exciting, and I felt a little stab of sadness that I had decided not to go. Had I passed up the chance of a lifetime . . . had I taken the wrong fork in the road?

I went back to the letter. "I'm still struggling with the language (wish you were here to help me!) but everyone has been so friendly, it doesn't seem to matter. Two of the French girls from L'Étoile are spending the whole day with me this Saturday. We're going to see some of the museums and monuments. Then we're going shopping in some boutiques, and in the evening we're going to a performance of *Sleeping Beauty*—my favorite ballet! Kerry, it's like a dream, a fairy-tale, and I still have to pinch myself sometimes to see if it's all real . . ."

Just then the phone rang, shattering my vision of tree-lined boulevards and marble statues, and I reluctantly put the letter aside.

"Hi, I wanted to thank you again for the horse."

"I love the medallion, too," I told Ian. "I'm wearing it right this minute."

"Good. I was hoping you'd wear it tonight, because I've got a big evening planned for us."

"You do?" Ian was always full of surprises.

"Have you ever heard of the Pasta Factory?"

"You're taking me to a factory?"

"No, it's a brand new restaurant in the Village where they have thirty-six different kinds of pasta! Everything from angel hair to spinach noodles."

I said with a laugh, "Ian, it sounds great, but after this why don't we start checking out all the wonderful health food restaurants in New York?"

"Oh, right. It's a deal. Anyway, the Pasta Factory

is just the beginning. This is Italian night. There's a new Italian movie I thought we could go to, and then we could finish up at Alfredo's for espresso. How does that sound?" He waited for me to say something.

"It sounds . . . fantastic," I said slowly. I felt as if his call had been an answer to my questions.

"You *do* want to go out with me tonight, don't you?" He sounded worried.

"More than you know," I told him.

"All right!" he said, sounding relieved. "I'll pick you up at six and we'll head down to the Pasta Factory right away."

After he hung up, I held the phone for a minute, thinking. Had I really taken the right path? Maybe, but I'd never know for sure . . .

One thing was certain, though. Paris would still be there waiting for me when I was ready. Ian was here and now.

## The End

*Ending 2 begins on the next page.*

# Ending 2

I looked into those wonderful eyes, and my carefully rehearsed speech fell apart. Ian was staring at me questioningly, so I took a deep breath and began.

"This is sort of a double celebration tonight," I said. I wanted my voice to be strong and confident, but it came out a thin croak. He waited for me to go on. "It's more than just the opening night of *Swan Lake*. Ian . . . something very important has happened to me." I paused, watching him. "I've been offered a scholarship."

"Kerry! That's fantastic. Isn't it kind of early to get a college scholarship, though? You're only a junior."

"It's not for college. It's a dance scholarship."

"That's terrific. Hey, I'm really proud of you." He moved closer and slid his arm around me. His eyes were glowing in the flickering candlelight, and he flashed one of his electric smiles. He gave my arm a squeeze, and I tried to ignore the exciting tingle that raced through me. "Where will you be going to school?"

"Paris."

The smile slowly drained from his face, as if someone had pulled a switch.

"Paris," he repeated softly. He gave me a searching look. "When?"

"Soon," I told him, forcing the word out. I felt like I was choking. There was a long silence. "Classes start in the middle of November, but I have to get over there earlier to get settled."

He still didn't say anything, and I heard myself talking too fast, the way I always do when I'm nervous. "I'll . . . I'll be staying at a pension—that's like a boardinghouse—with Jill, a girl I know from dance class. We'll spend half the day taking high school courses, and half the day at L'Étoile, the dance academy. We'll be there until May.

"It's a wonderful opportunity," I said in a strangled voice. "The chance to study with some of the greatest teachers in the world. A once-in-a-lifetime . . ." my voice trailed off, and I looked at him worriedly. Wasn't he ever going to say anything? He was staring at his hands as if he had never seen them before. I found myself staring at them, too. It seemed like a long time before he finally spoke.

"I'm happy for you, Kerry. Really." He exhaled slowly, as if he had been holding his breath. "I wish I could be totally unselfish and say that it's the best thing in the world for you . . . but I can't." He gave me a little smile and pulled me close to him for a minute. He ran his hand through my hair and tilted my chin back to look at me. "Oh, Kerry, I'm really going to miss you, you know?"

"I know," I gulped. A lump had started to rise in

my throat, and if I wasn't careful, I'd be crying in a matter of seconds.

"I had so many plans for us . . ." he began.

I remembered. Chinatown dinners. Browsing in Village bookstores on Saturday mornings. Long days at the ocean. Dozens of images flooded my mind—pictures of sunny days and exciting nights that were waiting for me with Ian. And I was throwing them all away.

I tried to compose myself, to steady my voice, before I began to speak. How could I make him understand? "Ian." I touched his cheek and he turned to me. "It's not the end, you know. I'll write to you from Paris. And . . . and I'll think about you every day."

He forced a dry laugh. "You're sure you won't fall for some slick Frenchman on a motorcycle who speeks like theese?" He did a terrible French accent.

"No, I won't." I smiled at him, and he kissed the tip of my nose.

"But what about all our plans . . . all the places I wanted to take you?"

"I'll just have to take a lot of rain checks. And I'm coming back in May."

He gave me a heartbreaking grin, just as the waitress brought us our dinners. They looked delicious. Yet again, Ian was introducing me to something new and wonderful.

"Promise?" Ian asked, his face just inches from my own.

"Promise."

I had dreaded telling Ian, but it was over so

quickly. It had been both better and worse than I expected. Better because we both had been so calm about it, worse because now I realized just how much I cared for him.

It was late when I got home, but Mom, Dad, and the Wizard were watching TV in the den. I had the feeling they were waiting for me.

"How did it go?" the Wizard asked, jumping to his feet.

"It was great," I said, smiling. "Six curtain calls." I sank into a chair, exhausted. "I can't wait for you all to come see it tomorrow night."

"I want to hear every detail," Mom said, "but let me fix us some cocoa first. And how about a few cookies?"

"Okay, that sounds good." Even though I had eaten with Ian, I felt ravenously hungry again.

"Not a word till I come back," she said, disappearing into the kitchen.

"We're all proud of you, Kerry," Dad said. We smiled at each other, and I realized with a pang how much I would miss the three of them.

"I told all the kids at school that you were dancing in New York tonight," the Wizard volunteered. "I kind of like having a sister who's a celebrity."

"Just a chorus dancer."

"Well, maybe today," Dad said. "But tomorrow— who knows?"

Mom came back with the cocoa then and insisted on hearing all about the show. I told her about the shimmering costumes, the amber gels that bathed the stage in a soft glow, the way the audience went wild at the end.

She listened with a little smile on her face and then said, "Did anything else happen tonight?"

"What do you mean?"

"Wasn't that Ian who dropped you off?"

I nodded. "He took me out to dinner after the show."

"You could have asked him in to help celebrate."

I let out a long breath. "Tonight's a special night," I said, "and I wanted to be alone with all of you."

"You've made up your mind," Mom said knowingly.

"Wow!" the Wizard exploded. "You have? Let me guess . . ."

"Daniel, please let Kerry tell us in her own way," Mom pleaded.

There was no point in prolonging the suspense. "I've decided to go to Paris," I blurted out.

"Whoopee!" the Wizard shouted, jumping up and down. "Now we'll get to come and visit you."

I had to smile. "I certainly hope so. That was part of the deal, wasn't it, Dad?" He nodded, and I said, "I don't think I could live till May without seeing everyone."

After a round of hugs and congratulations, Mom got out a pad and paper. "We have to start getting organized right away," she said, adjusting her reading glasses. "Do you know how much we have to do in such a short time?"

Dad and I smiled at each other. My mother is so organized, she makes lists of lists. "I think you two have a lot to talk over," he said, "and I see it's getting late. If you will excuse me, I need to read some briefs for tomorrow. And Daniel, it's time for you to call it a day."

"We need to work on your wardrobe," Mom went on, writing furiously. "You need some winter clothes and some good boots—it might be snowy there—and I want to get you a new suitcase. A nice lightweight one."

We stayed up talking until two o'clock in the morning. Then Mom looked at the clock and ushered me to bed. "You have a performance tomorrow night," she reminded me.

"As if I could forget," I teased her. I was achingly tired, more tired than I could ever remember being, and yet I felt keyed up, too excited to sleep. I tumbled into bed and lay awake thinking about the events of the evening. The magic of *Swan Lake* . . . Ian's face glowing in the candlelight . . . his funny French accent . . . his soft kiss. I'm giving him up, a little voice said inside me. But was I really? Couldn't we keep alive the deep feelings we had for each other? Or was I just kidding myself . . . would Ian forget me before my plane touched down in Paris?

I could only hope that I had made the right decision.

The next day was a Saturday, and I woke up late, a rare luxury. When I staggered downstairs, Mom was alone in the kitchen.

"Hi, sleepyhead. Do you want a late breakfast or an early lunch? Or better yet," she added, "why don't we try that new crepe place in town? We can get started on some shopping, too, unless you're too tired."

My legs felt like wet noodles, but I forced a smile.

"No, I'll be okay. I'll just have some tea and a quick shower. I don't have to be at the theater until seven, so we can take all afternoon."

We did.

We started with lunch at a restaurant called La Crêpe and sampled the specialty of the house— paper-thin crêpes filled with ham and mushrooms. They had dessert crêpes, too, and Mom tried to tempt me with a raspberry and whipped cream concoction, but I resisted.

"You're sure?" she said.

"Not unless you want to see a bloated swan tonight," I told her, grinning.

We compromised on café-au-lait, and Mom dragged out her foot-long list. There were a million details to arrange—details that I hadn't had time to think of. Plane tickets . . . tuition money . . . passport . . . a French bank account . . . Mom checked them off one by one.

"If we can just get most of the clothes taken care of today, we'll be in good shape," she said. "I spoke to Jill's mother this morning, and she said to be sure to stock up on sweaters. November is a cold month in Paris, and the nights are sure to be chilly."

I must have been quiet, because she turned to me suddenly. "Is anything wrong, Kerry? You have a funny look on your face."

"No, everything's fine," I assured her. "I guess it's just dawned on me that it's really going to happen—that I'm actually going to be living in Paris for a while. Going shopping just made it seem so . . . real, somehow."

She shot me a worried look. "Kerry, if you're not

sure, if you have any doubts . . . you can still change your mind. You know there's another option."

"No, it's not that," I told her. "This is really what I want to do—it's just that it seems so final."

We didn't say anything for a moment, and then I reached over and squeezed her hand. "You think I'm doing the right thing, don't you?" It was important for me to know.

She took a sip of coffee and put the cup down carefully. "I'm not sure it's a matter of the right thing versus the wrong thing, Kerry. No matter what choices you make in your life, there are always trade-offs—things you give up and things you get in return. But I do think you've made a good decision. This trip is something you'll always remember. And it will give you a chance to decide just how serious you are about your dancing.

"Anyway," she went on, "Easter will be here before you know it, and all of us will be together. You won't even have a chance to get homesick." She made some fierce slashes on the list. "Now," she said briskly, "let's make a start on your clothes. Do you think you'll be doing any skiing?"

The Air France jumbo jet circled lazily in the Paris sky, waiting for permission to land at Orly Airport. Jill was sitting in the window seat, calling out landmarks from her *Michelin Guide*.

"Look, Kerry, there's the Opera, and the Seine . . . that's Notre Dame. We really made it!"

It was snowing when we stepped out of the terminal, huge wet flakes that clung to our faces and hair. We hailed a taxi and Jill handed the driver a piece of paper with the address of our pension on it.

"At least taxi drivers are the same the world over," Jill said with a smile. We were careening down a wide boulevard at breakneck speed. I looked out the window and tried to orient myself, but it was impossible. It looked like every travel movie I had ever seen of Paris—except there was a thick blanket of snow covering everything. All the familiar sights passed in a blur—the Champs-Élysées . . . Montmartre . . . Sacre Coeur . . . rows of shops with names I struggled to remember from French class. *Boulangerie . . . pâtisserie . . . charcuterie.*

We screeched to a stop in front of a small, shabby building. "Are you sure this is it?" I asked Jill.

She spoke to the driver in halting French, and he grinned and reassured her. "*Oui, oui,*" he said. "*C'est ca.*" He deposited our suitcases in a pile of slush and took off in a cloud of exhaust fumes.

"Welcome to Paris," I muttered.

Moments later, Madame Rabant, our landlady, was beside us, clucking like a mother hen. "You are the Americans, yes? Come in, come in, you will catch the death of cold. You speak French, eh? *Parlez-vous français?* Not yet? Ah, *quel dommage.* Well, it will come in time."

She ushered us into a chilly parlor and served us coffee and cake. "The other students are not here yet, they are in the class. I have students from all countries," she said proudly. "Canadian, British, German, and one Spaniard, José," she added. "You will like them, all of them. I promise you."

She sat with us, smiling encouragingly at our

stumbling attempts at her language, and finally she stood up. "And now you excuse me, yes? I have to make the dinner."

One of the students showed us to our room. "I think we're going to like it here," I said to Jill, as we unpacked.

"I like it already," she answered, looking around the spacious room. It was simply but attractively furnished with two single beds, sturdy bookcases, and identical dressers. Closet space was scarce, but an enormous mahogany wardrobe stood in one corner.

"It's a good thing we didn't bring much," Jill moaned when we had filled the wardrobe. "Where will we put all these heavy sweaters?"

"Let's stash them in our suitcases and slide them under our beds," I suggested.

We had barely finished unpacking when Madame called us to dinner. "Come, come, meet the others," she said, leading us into the dining room. "Kerry and Jill from America," she said.

There was a chorus of greetings from around the table, mostly *bonjour*'s with a scattering of "his." As soon as we sat down, a plump, dark-haired girl named Leona spoke to me.

"We usually speak French during dinner," she said, "but since it's your first night here, we'll stick to English, if you prefer."

"That would help," I said gratefully. "Our French is pretty rusty."

"And yet you have a French . . . friend," she said, taking a closer look at my neck chain. On it was the medallion Ian had given me at the farewell party Mom had thrown for me.

"Oh, that!" My hand went to my throat self-consciously. "It was a going away present from an American friend. It has a French saying, though."

"I know," she said, smiling. "Quite a romantic line: *Plus qu'hier, moins que demain.* He must be a very special friend?"

"Very special," I said softly. I touched the medallion, with its beautiful saying: "More than yesterday, less than tomorrow." I felt a familiar sadness well up inside me. I had only been in Paris a few hours, and I missed Ian already.

Jill wanted to stay up talking with our new friends at the pension, but I decided to turn in early. The room seemed cold and lonely, dimly lit by an old-fashioned chandelier hung from a brass chain.

My first night in Paris I said to myself as I burrowed down under the covers, trying to get warm. For some reason, I didn't feel thrilled, just bone-tired and miles from home. Miles from Ian, too . . . I checked to make sure the medallion was on the night table where I had left it and snuggled back into the deep feather pillows.

I remembered how handsome Ian had looked at the farewell party. He had arrived early with a bunch of violets and the little jeweler's box that contained his gift . . .

"Violets in November?" I had exclaimed. Only Ian would think of that. He looked terrific in a pale blue sweater than accented his gray eyes.

By nine o'clock, the party was in full swing, and everyone was enjoying themselves. Shauna and I helped Mom dish out the spaghetti, and even Ian was pressed into service buttering thick slabs of Italian bread. I didn't get to talk to him as much as I wanted to, and before I knew it, the hours had slipped away.

At midnight we herded the last guest out the door, and Ian stood looking at me. "Want to go for a walk?" he asked. There was a soft, pleading look in his eyes. It was the last time we would see each other for months.

It was a chilly November night, with beads of moisture in the air. There were still some stars scattered in the sky, though, and Ian pointed out the constellations. "The Big Dipper . . . the Seven Sisters . . . Cassiopeia . . ." He leaned down to turn up the collar on my coat and gently kissed me. "After tomorrow, you'll be looking at the North Star from a different direction," he said.

"I'm sure it will look the same."

"Things might look different in Paris." We both knew he wasn't talking about stars. "Will you think of me sometimes?" he asked, wrapping his arm around my waist. "You won't forget me?"

"I won't forget you, Ian." I blinked quickly to hide the stinging tears that sprang to my eyes.

"Good. Because I'm not going to forget you, Kerry. And I'm going to be waiting right here for you in May."

A light rain started to fall, and we headed back to the house.

"I hate good-byes," he muttered, when we got to the front porch.

"Me too," I said in a little voice, fingering the precious medallion.

"There's only one thing that's good about them."

"What's that?"

"This." He gave me a lingering kiss that was so exciting I almost forgot to breathe. Finally he drew back and looked at me tenderly. "There's another one waiting for you when you get back, Kerry," he whispered.

Oh Ian, I thought, as tears welled up in my eyes. I miss you so much already! How will I ever make it until May without you?

I snuggled deep under the covers and tried to console myself with the thought that Ian had said he'd wait for me. The question was . . . for how long?

It was amazing how quickly things settled into a routine. The morning classes at the Institute weren't much different from my school work in Bronxville, except that I had an hour of French grammar and conversation every day.

The dance classes were strenuous, and I was glad now that Miss Beatrice had pushed us as hard as she had. Jill and I were above average in *pointe* work, and our teacher, Mademoiselle Mimi, commented on our technique.

"You must have had a teacher who is . . . how do you say, *rigoureux*. Rigorous, no?"

"Yes, very much so," I said, smiling at her. Miss Beatrice was certainly rigorous, I thought to myself.

Jill and I felt right at home at the studio. The tinkling piano music, the forest of leg-warmers and heavy woolen tights, the long wooden barre— everything was just as it had been at Miss Beatrice's. On the first day of class, we saw a beautiful young French girl slapping her ballet shoes against the door to soften them, just as we always did back in New York.

Jill burst out laughing. "What's that French saying: The more things change, the more they stay the same? There's living proof!"

One thing had definitely stayed the same: As the weeks went by, I continued to miss Ian. As I experimented with the new language, new food, humorous mistakes, and exciting discoveries, I thought of what he'd always told me when I hesitated over a menu or a destination: "Be adventurous." Ian always approached life like it was a wonderful adventure; he could turn an ordinary event into something magical.

Was Ian sharing adventures with someone else right this minute? I wondered one night as Jill and I were making hot chocolate to take upstairs to the chilly bedroom. Somehow, I couldn't picture Ian alone for very long. He was too full of life not to attract other people to him. Other girls . . .

"You still miss him, don't you?" Jill asked me, breaking into my thoughts.

"I sure do." Missing Ian was like a dull ache that never went away. Unconsciously, my hand went to my throat, and I touched the smooth medallion. "Something to remember me by," he had said. As if anyone could forget a boy like Ian.

Jill looked at me sympathetically as I shivered and pulled my sweater more tightly around me. If it got any colder, I was going to have to start wearing ski underwear every day.

"You're not going to turn into a hermit, are you?"

"What do you mean?" I asked, surprised.

"Well, you haven't exactly encouraged anyone from the pension to be friendly. Boys, I mean." She set out the cups and saucers and turned to face me. "José and Jean-Paul have asked us twice to go to Montmartre with them. They know all the student hangouts, all the fun spots. You know, there's one club that's fixed up like a cave. It's called the Pipistrello—that means bat in Italian—and it's supposed to be fabulous. I wish you'd reconsider going, Kerry."

"Jill, why don't you go with them?" I said quickly. "I told you I don't want you to stay home because of me."

"Kerry, don't you see? You shouldn't stay home, either. You haven't taken a vow, you know! We're in Paris—everything is right here, waiting for us to reach out and take it."

I smiled at her and tried to summon a little enthusiasm.

"I suppose you're right, José is really nice, and so is Jean-Paul, but—"

"But neither one is Ian."

"Exactly."

"Well, that doesn't mean you can't have a little bit of fun with them, you know," she said pointedly.

Later I lay in the freezing bedroom and watched the moon climb high in the Paris sky. On an impulse I threw on a robe and stood at the window. It was a dazzlingly clear night, and I searched the sky until I found the North Star. It looked exactly the same, and I smiled when I remembered Ian's words. Things might look different in Paris, he had warned me.

I could remember exactly the husky quality in his voice when he had said it, the way his arms slid around me, the soft pressure of his lips on mine.

You were wrong, Ian, I thought. Things are no different in Paris. I feel the same about you as I did in the States. The problem is, how do you feel about me? Will you really be waiting for me when I get back?

I stared blankly at the sky for a few minutes, too restless to sleep. I had always enjoyed scanning the sky with Ian, picking out constellations, learning bits of astronomy. Alone in Paris, the stars were mere pinpricks of light, cold and remote, and held no interest for me. I shivered and got back into bed.

I waited every day for a letter from Ian, and then suddenly it appeared, neatly tucked under my napkin at the breakfast table.

"Mail call," Jill said, smiling. "And I bet I know who it's from." I picked it up gingerly and put it into my pocket. "Aren't you going to read it?" she asked.

"I'll read it after breakfast," I muttered, embarrassed.

"Oh." She gave me an arch smile. "It's that serious, then?"

I made a face at her, then ate breakfast as quickly as I could. Afterwards, I managed to find a few minutes alone in the front parlor.

"*Ma cherie,*" it began. "*Allo! Bonjour!* I'd put on my best French accent, but I don't think it would come across too well on paper. I miss you so much! It seems like you've been gone for years instead of weeks." I smiled to myself because I understood exactly what he meant. "Whenever I see a girl with curly black hair, I think of you. And when I hear a song that we've danced to or listened to together, it drives me crazy! I haven't even been back to the Peking Palace because I knew the fried squid would remind me of you. Just kidding!

"Nothing is quite right here without you. Everything has closed in, the way it does when you look through the wrong end of a telescope. I went to Soho and Chinatown last Sunday, and they weren't the same.

"I've tried to picture what your life in Paris must be like. I know you're living in a pension, and I'm wondering if it's filled with great-looking guys with sexy accents who are trying to lure you away from me. I hope not! Because I'm counting on you coming right back to me in May, and we can pick up where we left off."

Oh, Ian, I thought. I think of you constantly, too! How could I have left you? I'd give anything if you were here with me now.

"I miss everything we did together—remember the picnics at the zoo, and those funny dinners in Chinatown? And the Cloisters on Sunday afternoons when we pretended we lived back in medieval times?

"I can't wait to see you again in May. And this time I'm going to hold on to you, so you can't get away!

"Take care of yourself. All my love, Ian."

It was a beautiful letter, and I had to brush away the quick tears that sprang to my eyes. Had I done the right thing in coming to Paris? As far as dancing was concerned, yes, I had made the right choice. But what about Ian?

My thoughts were interrupted when Jill popped into the room. "Finished reading your mash note from Ian?" I nodded and dropped the letter back in my pocket. "Well, I'll pester you for all the spicy details later, but right now, there's something much more urgent. José and Jean-Paul want to know if they can take us to the Pipistrello tonight. There's a really great band performing tonight, so they need to know right away so they can make a reservation. What do you say?"

I started to say something, and she held up her hand. "Before you tell me, just remember that I won't take no for an answer." Her tone was teasing, but I had the feeling that she meant it.

"Please, Kerry," she said. "You have to start enjoying Paris sometime. If nothing else, it will make the time go quicker until May."

"Okay, you win," I finally told her. "Tell José and Jean-Paul that we'd love to go with them."

She gave me a big smile and I was suddenly glad that I had relented. "Okay, I'll be right back," she said, and disappeared into the kitchen.

My hand closed protectively over the letter in my pocket. Later, I wanted to read it over and over again in my room. I wanted to think about Ian and relive all the wonderful times we had had together. Mostly, I wanted to savor every word and believe that he really would be waiting for me in May.

But for the moment, Jill was right. I was in Paris, and the whole city was waiting for me to reach out and grab it.

## The End

Here's an exciting excerpt from
FRIENDS FOREVER, the first book in the
TURNING POINTS series—a romance
with two endings . . . which one would
you choose?


# TURNING POINTS #1: FRIENDS FOREVER
### by Lisa Norby


WANTED: 5 FRESHMAN CHEERLEADERS
PRELIMINARY TRYOUT—THURSDAY AFTERNOON, 3:30
DO YOU HAVE WHAT IT TAKES?

Well, why not? Laura wondered. Of course, Katie was probably
right that her chances of being chosen were nil. But what did she
have to lose? Why not show up for the preliminary audition? At
the very least it would be serving notice to Steffie that she wasn't
just another mousy freshman afraid of competing with the senior
cheerleading captain.

The thought had hardly formed itself in her mind when Laura
realized that there was one major problem with her plan. Katie.
If Katie knew that she was planning to go to the tryout, she
would be sure to put down the idea so thoroughly that Laura
would chicken out and change her mind before Thursday ever
came around. Katie didn't mean to be unsupportive; it was just
that she was, well, a bit too blunt about putting her thoughts into
words. It would be easier just to say nothing. Then, when the
audition came to nothing, as chances were it would, Katie would
never have to know.

It was a wonderful plan except for one small thing. Deep
down inside her, Laura could hear the whispery voice of her
conscience calling her a coward. If she didn't have the nerve to
confide her plan to her best friend, then how was she ever going
to make an impression on the rest of the world?

It was a good question, but Laura decided for the moment to
ignore it. There was such a thing as being too logical. Sometimes
it seemed as if that was Katie's problem. Just for once she was
going to go her own way and not ask Katie's approval. All she had
to do was think of a way to keep Katie from finding out . . . .

# SIGNET VISTA Books You'll Enjoy

## JOIN THE *TURNING POINTS* READER'S PANEL

Help us bring you more and better books by filling out this survey and mailing it in today.

1. Book title:_____

   Book #:_____

2. Using the scale below, how would you rate this book on the following features? Please write in one rating from 0-10 for each feature in the spaces provided.

|  | | NOT SO GOOD | | | O.K. | | | GOOD | | EXCEL-LENT |
|---|---|---|---|---|---|---|---|---|---|---|
| POOR | | | | | | | | | | |
| 0 | 1 | 2 | 3 | 4 | 5 | 6 | 7 | 8 | 9 | 10 |

*RATING*

Overall opinion of book........................ _____
Story .................................... _____
Conclusion/endings
       #1 .................................. _____
       #2 .................................. _____
Main characters
       Hero ............................... _____
       Heroine ............................ _____
Scene on front cover...................... _____
Colors of front cover..................... _____

3. Listed below are different young adult romance series. Rate only those you have read using the 0-10 scale below.

|  | | NOT SO GOOD | | | O.K. | | | GOOD | | EXCEL-LENT |
|---|---|---|---|---|---|---|---|---|---|---|
| POOR | | | | | | | | | | |
| 0 | 1 | 2 | 3 | 4 | 5 | 6 | 7 | 8 | 9 | 10 |

*RATING*

SWEET DREAMS ........................... _____
FIRST LOVE .............................. _____
WILDFIRE ................................ _____
CAPRICE ................................. _____
TURNING POINTS .......................... _____
TWO-BY-TWO ............................ _____
FOLLOW YOUR HEART ..................... _____
YOUNG LOVE ............................. _____
MAKE YOUR DREAMS COME TRUE .......... _____
_____ _____
_____ .................. _____

4. How likely are you to buy another title in the Turning Points Series? (Circle one number on scale below.)

| DEFI-NITELY NOT BUY | PROB-ABLY NOT BUY | | NOT SURE | | PROB-ABLY BUY | DEFI-NITELY BUY |
|---|---|---|---|---|---|---|
| 0 | 1 | 2 | 3 | 4 | 5 | 6 | 7 | 8 | 9 | 10 |

5. Where did you get this book?
   ( ) Bought it            ( ) Borrowed it from a friend
   ( ) School library       ( ) Received it as a gift
   ( ) Public library       ( ) Other:_____

6. Where do you usually buy your books (check one or more):
   ( ) Bookstore            ( ) School Book Club
   ( ) Supermarket          ( ) Discount Store
   ( ) Variety Store        ( ) Department Store
   ( ) Drug Store           ( ) Other:_____
   ( ) School book fair

7. What is your age? _____      Sex: ( ) Male
                                          ( ) Female

8. About how many young adult romance books have you bought for yourself in the last six months?

                Approximate #: _____

9. What are the names of two of your favorite magazines?

        1) _____

        2) _____

If you would like to participate in future research projects, please, please complete the following:

PRINT NAME:_____

ADDRESS:_____

CITY:_____STATE_____ZIP_____

PHONE: (      )_____

Thank you. Please send to New American Library, Young Adult Research Department, 1633 Broadway, New York, New York 10019.